"Has my identity been compromised?"

"Not that I'm aware of. But I'm here to take you back to Mustang Ridge."

"You can't take me back there, Jake. It's too dangerous."

"I don't want to harm you."

She wasn't sure she believed that—Jake had good reason to want to do her harm. If only Maggie could go back in time three years....

"If you're not taking me to the man who put me in WITSEC, then where are you taking me?"

"To the hospital for some tests. After that, I'll let you go."

The hospital? "But I'm not sick."

Maggie stopped. What would make Jake McCall come all this way to take her to Mustang Ridge for some tests?

There was only one thing.

Sunny.

She reached across the seat and latched onto his jacket, wadding up the fabric in her fists. "What's wrong? What happened to my niece?"

USA TODAY Bestselling Author

DELORES FOSSEN

CHRISTMAS RESCUE AT MUSTANG RIDGE

HARLEQUIN®
entertain, enrich, inspire™

Recycling programs
for this product may
not exist in your area.

ISBN-13: 978-0-373-69656-7

CHRISTMAS RESCUE AT MUSTANG RIDGE

ABOUT THE AUTHOR

Imagine a family tree that includes Texas cowboys, Choctaw and Cherokee Indians, a Louisiana pirate and a Scottish rebel who battled side by side with William Wallace. With ancestors like that, it's easy to understand why *USA TODAY* bestselling author and former air force captain Delores Fossen feels as if she were genetically predisposed to writing romances. Along the way to fulfilling her DNA destiny, Delores married an air force top gun who just happens to be of Viking descent. With all those romantic bases covered, she doesn't have to look too far for inspiration.

Books by Delores Fossen

HARLEQUIN INTRIGUE

*Five-Alarm Babies
**Texas Paternity
‡Texas Paternity: Boots and Booties
‡‡Texas Maternity: Hostages
††Texas Maternity: Labor and Delivery
***The Lawmen of Silver Creek Ranch

CAST OF CHARACTERS

Sheriff Jake McCall—He's willing to do anything to save his daughter's life, and that includes finding his former sister-in-law, the woman he blames for his wife's death. But Jake's life isn't the only thing he'll have to risk. He'll have to risk his heart, as well.

Maggie Gallagher—Once a tough-as-nails cop, she becomes a killer's target, and the one man who can rescue her is Jake McCall. However, Jake comes with the ultimate strings attached, because falling for him means they first have to stay alive.

Sunny Lynn McCall—Jake's three-year-old daughter. She's too young to realize the danger and the steps her daddy has taken to save her.

Deputy Royce McCall—Even though he doesn't welcome Maggie back with open arms, he'll do whatever it takes to help his brother protect her.

Chet McCall—Jake's father, who might be willing to deal with his enemies to get back at Maggie.

Bruce Tanner—He's on death row for killing Jake's wife, but he could still be calling the shots from his prison cell.

Wade Garfield—The computer tech who helped Jake but might also have betrayed him.

David Tanner—Bruce Tanner's son. He claims he's a changed man, but is it all a ruse to help his father?

Dr. Gavin Grange—The once-trusted town doctor, he could now be on a killer's payroll.

Chapter One

Sheriff Jake McCall knew what he was about to do could put a woman in grave danger. Maybe even get her killed. He wasn't certain he could live with that, but he sure as hell couldn't live with the alternative, either.

Risking Maggie Gallagher's life, and his, was the only choice he had.

He pushed the stallion hard, its hooves chopping into the frozen ground. The icy wind whipped at him and burned his eyes and hands. But he rode harder. Away from the ranch house and away from what was waiting for him there.

It didn't help.

Jake had known that when he saddled up, but he couldn't face what was inside. Not yet. Though delaying it didn't change the fact that he'd have to do things he had sworn he'd never do.

Like see *Maggie* again.

He hated her more than he wanted her. Far more. And he hated himself for still wanting her after what had happened. That settled like a deadweight in Jake's gut, and he figured that particular feeling wasn't going to get better anytime soon.

Cursing, Jake pushed that thought aside and rode the half mile to the creek, not stopping, not slowing until he got to the ice-scabbed water's edge. He reined in the stallion, put his thumb to the brim of his Stetson to ease it back a bit, and he sat there, his forearm on the saddle horn.

He stared out at the glassy black surface of the creek and at the cottonwood trees, all veiny and bare. In the thin white moonlight he glanced down at the silver star badge pinned to his denim shirt pocket and felt a pain of a different kind. The badge meant something to him. Always had. It was his anchor. His cause.

Him.

Yeah, that was a sappy cliché that he'd never admit aloud. Not here in rural Texas where the only acceptable feelings for a real man to show were anger, appreciation for good-looking women and love for animals and small children.

But it was true.

People didn't call him Boy Scout for nothing.

The stallion snorted, its breath mixing with the air and creating a milky haze around them. He looked back at Jake with a judgmental dark eye and snorted again.

It was too butt-freezing cold to be out on this December night trying to ride off his troubles. But he'd wanted one last look at the place, just in case he never saw it again.

Jake gathered the reins, maneuvered the stallion around and headed back. No gallop this time. He kept the stallion's gait easy and slow, but each step still took him home.

There were twinkling lights around the windows. A holly wreath on the door. A plastic Santa and his sleigh perched on the roof. It still didn't feel like Christmastime even though it was only three days away.

Jake spotted his brother, Royce, on the porch that ran across the entire front of the ranch house. Royce was on the top step, his lanky jeans-clad legs stretched out in front of him while he took a long drag on a cigarette.

Since Royce had quit smoking some four years ago, it was a reminder to Jake that he wasn't the only one in for a bad night. Royce flicked the cigarette into what was left of their sister's petunia bed. She'd complain about that come spring when she found it.

By then, all of their lives here would have changed.

One way or another.

"Dad's waiting on you." Royce got up from the step, the Christmas lights flickering off the silver deputy's badge he had clipped to his rawhide belt. "You okay?" Royce asked.

"No." Jake figured a lie would just stick in his throat so he didn't even try it.

His brother stopped a moment as if considering that, and then he made a sound that could have meant anything before he strolled inside.

Jake dismounted and led the stallion to the barn. He mumbled an apology for the hard ride while he took off the saddle and gave the horse a quick brush down. He hurried now, dreading the delay more than he dreaded the conversation that was about to take place, and Jake made his way back to the house.

The moment he opened the door, he spotted them in the great room that sprawled out in front of him.

Family.

His brother, Royce. His sister, Nell. His father, Chet.

Royce had already taken the chair near the fireplace where a stack of mesquite logs were crackling and spitting. Chet was in his leather recliner that was positioned like a throne, the toes of his black snakeskin boots aimed at the ceiling. Jake spared him a glance before he went to the room across the hall. It'd once been a guest room, but these days it was more of a home-hospital for his daughter.

Sunny Lynn McCall.

She owned every bit of Jake's heart.

Jake didn't go in. He watched from the doorway as the visiting nurse, Betsy Becker, gave his daughter another injection. His little girl barely moved, didn't even open her eyes, despite the needle being jammed into her hip.

That nearly brought Jake to his knees.

Three years old was way too young to be immune to pain. Too young to die. It was up to him now to make sure that didn't happen.

Betsy took off her surgical mask, came out of the room and dodged Jake's gaze. "I'm sorry. I'll be back in the morning." She gave him a pat on the arm.

Betsy didn't linger, didn't speak to the others. She was a fixture now, appearing at the ranch every morning and leaving every night. She grabbed her things and let herself out. Jake had no doubts that come seven in the morning Betsy would be back to shove more needles into his baby.

Sometimes life just plain sucked, but it was easier to take a kick in the teeth when he was on the receiving end of the pain. Watching Sunny suffer like this was a special form of hell that he wouldn't wish on anyone.

Well, maybe there was someone.

He pulled in a long breath, went into the adjoining bathroom so he could scrub up and put on a surgical mask. He wasn't sick, but they couldn't take any chances with Sunny.

When Jake walked to her bed, Sunny didn't wake up and probably wouldn't, because lately she was more tired than not. He leaned down, kissed both cheeks, ran his fingers through her dark hair. He lingered a bit despite hearing Chet impatiently clear his throat.

The room was as cheerful as Jake had been able to make it. The floor-to-ceiling Christmas tree in the corner was decorated with lights and angel ornaments that Sunny had picked out from an online catalog. Her stuffed animals and dolls were nearby. Coloring books, too.

"You gonna make us wait all night?" Chet snarled.

Chet always sounded as if he was picking a fight. Except when he talked to Sunny. Jake's baby girl had wrapped her grandpa around her pinkie and vice versa. And that was the reason that Jake could still love his dad.

Of course, Jake didn't *like* him much, but that wasn't likely to change.

Jake gave Sunny another kiss, gently squeezed her hand and took off his mask so he could face his family.

"I'll stay with Sunny while you *talk,*" Nell whispered. His sister didn't know what was up, but Jake knew she would always step in to take care of her niece.

He was counting heavily on that.

"Well?" Chet, again. Another snarl. "Did you find *her?*"

Jake waited until Nell had closed the door to Sunny's room before he answered Chet's questions. "I found her. More or less."

Royce knew where this was going, and that was no doubt why he cursed and probably wished he had another smoke or two. "She's in the Witness Security Program."

"She's where?" Chet snapped.

"WITSEC, witness security," Jake supplied, though Chet had no doubt heard him the first time. The man was sixty-four, but there was nothing wrong with his hearing. Or his mind. "She was placed in the program after, well, just *after,*" Jake settled for saying.

Chet cursed. "The marshals won't tell you where she is." It wasn't a question, and it was followed by more cursing.

Royce took up the explanation since he'd been at the sheriff's office when Jake had gotten the news. "We sent a request all the way up to the head of WITSEC, but our request was denied."

Chet got to his feet and started to pace. "If I could get my hands around her neck—"

"She probably doesn't know Sunny's sick," Jake interrupted. "And we don't know if it'll be worth it to even find her."

That was the hardest part of all.

This could all be for nothing.

"I don't know how much the Justice Department is telling her because—" Jake had to pause and breathe "—it could be dangerous if anyone found out her new identity and her location."

"Damn right it's dangerous," Chet snapped. "It's dangerous for Sunny, too. And if *she* can help, then I don't care about compromising her identity. Hell, I don't care if somebody guns her down like—"

Thankfully, Chet had the good sense to stop. Jake already had enough bad things to deal with tonight without the memories of his late wife's murder. Of course, the memories of Anna were there.

Always.

Even though she'd been dead and buried for over two and a half years now, since Sunny was just a baby.

"Are we just going to keep calling her *she* and *her?*" Royce asked. He huffed, but Jake didn't know if he was just riled about the situation or the pronoun use. "Because she's got a name, you know?"

"Yeah, and it's a name not welcome here," Chet insisted.

His father wasn't the forgive-and-forget sort.

Neither was Jake in this situation.

But Sunny needed her. And that meant Jake needed her, too.

"Maggie Gallagher," Jake said aloud. It was the first time that name had crossed his lips in two years, eight months and five days.

Maggie, his former sister-in-law. Or would that be his

late wife's sister? Or how about the woman who'd gotten Anna killed? Yeah, that was the label that fit her best.

Maybe Chet had the right idea about not saying her name.

Chet stopped pacing and snapped toward Jake. "How you gonna convince those marshals to give us her location?"

The million-dollar question. Jake had a fifty-cent answer.

Jake shook his head. "I can't convince them. Royce and I have already tried."

"We have," Royce agreed. He glanced at Chet. "The Justice Department can't tell us where she is because during her relocation processing, Maggie specifically said she didn't want contact with any of us."

Chet cursed again.

If Jake had been feeling charitable—he wasn't—he would have pointed out that Chet had warned Maggie that if she ever came back to Mustang Ridge, he'd kill her and the horse she rode in on. Hardly a welcome-mat greeting. And it was that threat that had no doubt caused Maggie to include the no-contact order.

Chet lifted his hands, palms up. "So, that's it? You're just gonna give up?"

It took Jake a moment to rein in his voice. "I'll never give up."

Chet shook his head, riffled his hand through his hair. "Then *never giving up* better come with some kind of plan attached."

"I have a plan," Jake managed to say. It wasn't a good one, though, and it would hurt.

Oh, yeah. It'd hurt *bad*.

"Best if I don't give you any details of what I have to do." Jake unpinned his badge and dropped it on the table.

It hardly made it sound when it hit the soft pinewood.

Funny, he figured it would. Because the sound sure went through him. That badge was fourteen years of his life and had been pinned to his pockets since he was twenty-one.

"For safekeeping," Jake explained, knowing as explanations went, that it wasn't a very good one.

Or an honest one.

Chet glared at the badge, then at Jake. "We're family. We got a right to know what you're doing."

Jake pulled in a weary breath, shook his head and started for the door.

Chet called out for him to stop, but Jake just kept going. There was no way he could tell his family that come tomorrow, all hell was going to break loose.

And that he, Sheriff Jake McCall, was about to become an outlaw.

Chapter Two

There had been a time in her life when Maggie Gallagher would have knocked a man senseless for pinching her butt.

Now wasn't that time.

Maggie ignored the gesture that Herman Settler probably thought was good ol' boy friendly fun, and she deposited the plate in front of him.

Flop two, over hard. Smeared raft on the side.

Or in nondiner lingo: fried eggs and buttered toast.

The lingo was all mixed up in her head now. Mixed up with things like Herman's butt pinch and the squirrel-brown uniform she wore five days a week. Sometimes six. It wasn't normal. It wasn't good. But Maggie didn't fight it.

She hadn't fought it or anything else in a long time.

"Top off my coffee, darlin'," Herman drawled, and added a wink. Flirting with her.

Didn't the man realize he was old enough to be her father? Her boss, Gene Dayton, sure did. Gene was busy frying more eggs and sausages on the grill, but even through the haze of griddle smoke and grease splattering, Gene still managed to give Herman a look that could have frozen the hottest part of Hades.

Later, Gene would lecture her about letting men like Herman run roughshod over her.

And he'd actually use the word *roughshod*.

She'd nod, pretend to agree. Pretend that it mattered. Because it was easier than explaining why she wasn't looking for a fight. Not with Herman. Not with Gene.

Especially not with herself.

She reached across the tiled counter for the coffeepot. The tile was a dingy yellow now with even dingier hairline cracks running through it. Still, it was clean. Maggie should know since she'd been the one to clean it. It was the part of her job she liked best.

The only part, she amended.

The bell jingled over the door as she was topping off Herman's coffee. Maggie looked at the wall clock, not the glass door. Ten twenty-three. The bell ringer would be Ted Halvert, owner of the town's newspaper, the *Coopersville Crier*.

Ted was a few minutes early, but he was the only customer Maggie was expecting this time of day. For most people, it was already too late for breakfast, too early for lunch, and the Tip Top didn't have enough ambience for people to drop by for just coffee or conversation.

"Got your table ready, Ted." Maggie leaned back over the counter to set down the coffeepot, turned to give Ted the smile he would expect.

The smile froze on her face.

And the pot slammed on the dingy tile that she'd just cleaned.

The sound of the breaking glass registered in Maggie's mind, but something else took over. Another set of lingo. A different set of rules.

She reached for a gun that she no longer wore.

Her riffling hand slid right across the shoulder holster that wasn't there, either.

"Megan?" Gene called out. "You okay?"

It was her name now. Megan Greer. Her "relocation"

name that had become second nature like cleaning and fake smiles, but Maggie couldn't process it or Gene's question.

Her breath stalled in her lungs. The blood rushed to her head. And everything she'd put behind her, everything she'd tried to choke down in a deep dark place, all of it came crashing back.

Because of Sheriff Jake McCall.

It was him all right. All six feet, three inches of him. Standing there in the tinsel-decorated doorway of the Tip Top, glaring at her from the brim of a black Stetson. Beneath his buckskin shearling coat, Maggie saw the shoulder holster.

A real one.

And Jake's hand was on the butt of that real Colt .45.

"Are you here to finish things?" Maggie whispered. Not much sound in her voice, and everything inside her began to fall apart.

Unlike Jake.

He stood there, unmoving and unruffled, those Winchester-blue eyes drilling holes in her. Now, here was a man who could ride roughshod over her.

And she would deserve it.

"Megan?" Gene called out again.

Everyone had their eyes trained on Jake and her, and even though Maggie's eyes were on Jake, she knew Herman was already putting his hand on the little Smith & Wesson he carried in the slide holster in the back of his jeans.

And he'd draw it.

Gene, too.

Even though Jake looked, smelled and acted like a cowboy cop, his mute reaction, the outlaw stubble and narrowed bloodshot eyes would alarm everyone. It wouldn't be long before Gene pulled the Saturday night special he kept by the cash register. He didn't know how to use it, but that wouldn't stop him from trying to protect her.

Maggie had to do something to defuse the situation, or soon bullets might start flying.

"I'm okay," Maggie gutted out. She forced a smile. God, that was hard because her jaw muscles had frozen. "This is an old friend."

That was hard, too. And it lit a bad angry fire in Jake's eyes. Because they weren't friends any longer. And there was little chance of her ever making it happen again.

Especially since he'd likely snapped and come here to kill her.

She'd had nightmares about it, of course, but hadn't thought it would actually come down to it. Jake wasn't the sort to take the law into his own hands. He definitely wasn't a killer, but after what'd happened to Anna—her sister—Maggie wasn't sure what sort of man he was these days.

Maggie peeled off her apron, hoping no one noticed that her hands were shaking like crazy, and she grabbed her coat from the wooden peg on the back wall. She tossed the apron on the hook, missed but didn't pick it up. Too many steps to process and there were more important steps now.

"I'm going on my break," she called out to Gene, and didn't wait for him to challenge that. "Let's take this outside," Maggie added in a whisper meant only for Jake's ears.

Since she wasn't sure Jake would go for her suggestion, she risked hooking her arm through his. He wasn't shaking like her, but he was cold, making her wonder how long he'd stood out there watching her.

Plotting and planning what he wanted to do to her.

The question was—would Maggie let him do those things?

Possibly.

Jake wasn't the only wounded soul who was sick and tired of dealing with the aftermath of what had once been a life.

A blast of icy air slammed into her when she opened the door, and the silver-colored bells on the tacky plastic holly wreath jangled and jumped. Maggie said a quick prayer that Jake would budge, and she cursed herself for not having prayed sooner. Because it worked.

Jake budged.

And he walked out into the bitter cold with her.

"This way," he growled, and he took the lead, heading toward the parking lot. No snow, but the steely clouds overhead looked threatening.

"Thanks," she mumbled. They passed Ted, who was heading into the diner for his usual late breakfast. "There are a lot of good people inside. I didn't want them hurt."

"My fight's not with them," Jake mumbled back.

Maggie would have had to be deaf or unconscious not to react to that. Or to Jake himself. Her former brother-in-law was a formidable man and had a way of taking over a room just by stepping into it. Tall, dark and intimidating.

Once, she'd been crazy in love with him.

Well, maybe not in love exactly.

In lust with him for sure, as every Mustang Ridge female over the age of thirteen had been. Her sister had once said that Jake could stop a man's heart in midbeat. Or send a woman's heart racing.

Maggie had experienced both at one time or another.

She remembered their one and only kiss. She could still taste him, could still feel his rough cowboy hands and mouth on her.

Something Jake had warned her to forget.

Right.

She hadn't had much luck with that.

And he'd dismissed the kiss and the body contact against the barn wall as part of the grief of recently losing his wife. Maggie had dismissed it, too. Then, they'd learned Anna's death was Maggie's fault, in part anyway, and the dismissing turned to rage for Jake.

The rage was still there.

She could feel it as strongly as she could feel the kiss that she was supposed to forget.

"How'd you find me?" she asked.

His arm tensed, and he slung off her grip as if she'd scalded him. Or maybe he just remembered how much it disgusted him to touch her.

Or answer her.

Because Jake ignored her question.

He reached in his pocket and used his keypad to unlock the doors of a dark blue F-150 truck. He put her in first, practically shoving her into the passenger's seat. Jake didn't even glance at her as he walked in front of the truck so he could climb behind the wheel. He probably figured she wasn't going to run, especially since she'd coaxed him out of the diner.

"You're going to shoot me in your truck?" she asked, glancing at the pristine exterior. "It'd be a heck of a mess to clean up."

She was pleased and surprised that it sounded smart-mouthed. Better than letting him know she was so scared that she was about to lose her breakfast.

Something else that'd need cleaning.

The image of that hit Maggie the wrong way, and a short burst of air left her mouth. Definitely not a laugh. All nerves. And then the stupid tears came, burning her eyes and forcing her to choke them back.

"You couldn't hate me any more than I hate myself," Maggie said, and she swiped away a tear.

Now, she got him looking at her. Jake turned those lethal cop's eyes on her. "Don't bet on that."

The answer was actually a relief. Old lingo kicked in. Old training, too. If she could get him talking, maybe she could...what?

Talk him out of this?

Calm him down?

Make him see it was a mistake to come here?

Maggie wasn't sure that was the fair thing to do. Or if she could do it at all. Once upon a time she'd thought she could do anything.

She'd been stupid.

And now that stupidity was catching up with her. She could only shrug at that and concede that she was due. For two years, eight months and six days, she'd been living on borrowed time and mercy.

Maggie looked at him. Looked outside. Waited. And felt the goose bumps riffle over her entire body. Sweet heaven. Her coat wasn't thick enough, but she pulled the sides together, hunched her shoulders.

"How's Sunny?" she risked asking.

And she braced herself for him to reach for his gun. Right before his father, Chet, had run her out of Mustang Ridge, Jake warned her never to say his daughter's name. That was a McCall thing. If you crossed them—Jake's siblings or Chet—your name was mud.

Hers was something lower than mud.

Of course, Jake didn't answer her. He wouldn't give her that much, and if their situations had been reversed, Maggie probably wouldn't have, either.

"So, what? We just sit here mute as monkeys and freeze to death?" she asked. Her voice was quivering now, and she didn't know how much longer she could keep up this act of someone who wasn't about to go nuts. "At least it wouldn't require much cleanup."

That deepened his scowl. "I figured you'd be working as a cop."

"No." And that's all Maggie could manage for several seconds. "I gave up my badge and went with another career choice."

He looked at the peeling painted sign on the side of the building. "Waitress at the Tip Top Diner."

Ah, two could go in the smart-mouthed direction.

"Fewer things to screw up at a diner," she settled for saying.

Jake's forehead bunched up, and he nodded. Just nodded.

It hit her then. Maybe he wasn't there to kill her after all. Maybe he'd come to warn her, though she couldn't think of a good reason why he'd be the one to do that.

"Has my identity been compromised?" She couldn't get the question out fast enough, and Maggie fired glances all around. The next question, however, didn't come easily. "Does Tanner know where I am?"

Bruce Tanner. The man who'd hired someone to gun down her sister to get back at Maggie for conducting an investigation into his multiple wrongdoings. He was in jail on death row now, but that didn't mean he couldn't find a way to kill her.

Get in line.

A lot of people wanted her dead.

"Tanner doesn't know," Jake said. "At least I don't think he does." With his hands bracketed on the steering wheel, Jake turned his head and nailed his gaze to hers. "I'm here to take you back to Mustang Ridge."

Maggie had anticipated Jake saying a lot of things, but that wasn't one of them. "Wh-what?"

"Mustang Ridge," Jake said as if that clarified everything. He started the engine and probably would have driven away if Maggie hadn't latched on to his wrist.

"You can't take me back there, Jake. It's too dangerous."

He looked at her as if she'd spouted a third eye. "You thought I'd come here to kill you, remember?"

"Yeah, but in hot blood. As in the emotion had taken over so that you weren't thinking straight. Taking me back to the one place where someone will see me and tell Tanner is premeditation—"

"I don't want to harm you." Jake cursed. "I don't want to harm you *today*," he quickly amended.

She wasn't sure she believed that, and Jake had good reason to want to do her harm. If Maggie could go back to three years ago, she would have never started that investigation into Bruce Tanner, the rancher who was as corrupt as he was rich and powerful. But Maggie had been eager for justice. Equally eager to make a name for herself in the Amarillo P.D. She'd wanted to bring Tanner down.

And she had succeeded in part.

Maggie had found the evidence necessary to arrest him for money laundering through real estate deals, and in retaliation, Tanner had hired someone to shoot and kill Anna in what was supposed to look like a foiled robbery attempt at a store where she'd been shopping.

Yes, eventually Maggie and her fellow officers had managed to pin the murder on Tanner and had put him on death row, but it hadn't brought back her sister. It hadn't eased Jake's hatred of her.

And it hadn't eased her hatred of herself.

"If you're not taking me to Tanner," she asked, "then where are you taking me?"

"To the hospital for some tests. After that, I'll let you go."

The hospital? "But I'm not sick."

Maggie stopped. What the heck would make Jake Mc-Call come all this way to take her to Mustang Ridge for some tests?

There was only one thing.

Sunny.

She reached across the seat and gripped on to his jacket, wadding up the fabric in her fists. "What's wrong? What happened to my niece?"

Maggie would have added more questions, but the sound of the sirens stopped her cold. It wasn't a sound she heard often in Coopersville.

The sirens didn't stop Jake, however. He threw the truck into gear.

"Put your seat belt on," Jake growled.

And that was the only warning Maggie got before Jake gunned the engine, and the truck barreled out of the parking lot.

Chapter Three

Jake tried not to react to the sirens wailing behind him. And he reminded himself that the local cops probably wouldn't be after him yet.

Probably.

But even if they were, he still had to get Maggie out of there.

"You've lost your mind," Maggie concluded.

She put on her seat belt as he'd ordered, though Jake wasn't sure how she managed it with her hands shaking that hard. She was chewing on her bottom lip, too, and there wasn't much color in her face.

He hadn't wanted to scare her.

Okay, maybe he had.

Fear was better than other things she could have chosen to do.

Like fight back.

Maggie had once been an Amarillo city cop with a good aim and a kick-butt attitude, and Jake had been surprised when she hadn't pulled a gun on him and tried to defend herself. But no. She'd confused things even more by going with him and poking fun at the fact that this could have been her last few moments on earth.

She pushed her dark blond hair from her face, looked

over her shoulder and no doubt saw the Coopersville police cruiser behind them. Not close.

And it wasn't exactly following them.

The cruiser pulled into the parking lot of the diner, and Jake kept going. He had to get out of there before the local sheriff realized that Maggie was gone.

"Are you planning to let me in on what's going on?" Maggie asked.

Not really. But he needed her cooperation and that meant he had to tell her at least some of the truth. It was a gamble, but Jake was feeling a little better about his chances since Maggie had already asked about Sunny. Maybe that meant she hadn't written off her niece.

Maybe that also meant she'd help with Jake's plan.

"Should I be screaming and trying to flag down Sheriff Myers?" she pushed.

Oh, yeah. She probably should, but Jake kept that to himself. "I hacked into the Justice Department database to find you."

"What?" She made a sound of pure outrage. "Why would you do something stupid like that? You know what could happen to me."

She stopped.

"Oh, I get it." Maggie huffed. "This is some kind of death by proxy thing. You lead one of Tanner's goons to me so he can kill me. Yeah, you'll lose your badge for hacking into the database. Maybe even spend some time in jail or on probation. But you'll have your McCall justice, and I'll be dead."

None of that was true. But he was glad Chet hadn't thought of it. Jake didn't think even his father would stoop that low, but with Chet, you never knew.

Jake turned onto a back road before he continued. "Sunny's sick."

Maggie froze and studied him a moment. "What's wrong with her?" Her voice was tentative. As if she didn't want to hear the answer.

Jake had practiced this part so it would sound sterile. "Aplastic anemia. Her bone marrow isn't producing enough new cells to keep her alive."

"Oh, God." And Maggie repeated it until it strung together like one syllable.

Jake gave her some time to try to absorb that. He wished her luck with it. He'd had several months now and was still trying to absorb it. It didn't make sense that his baby girl would have to fight for her life this way.

"How bad is it?" Maggie asked.

"Bad." He had to pause, take a deep breath. He'd rehearsed this part, too, but it still sickened him to say it. "She needs a bone marrow transplant fast. We've all had blood tests, and none of us match."

She repeated that, too. "And I'm a match?"

He glanced at her and met her gaze. "I hope."

"You don't know?" Her grip melted off him. "That's what the test is for, Jake, you didn't have to kidnap me. I would have done the test."

Her eagerness to help Sunny didn't ease the knot in his gut. That's because he was bargaining with the devil here.

A devil he'd kissed.

And dreamed about.

Hell, the dreams were the worst part, because in them he'd done a lot more than just kiss her. That made him one sick puppy.

"You had a no-contact clause in your relocation records," he reminded her. "The only way I could find you was to go into the database."

"Okay." She nodded, stayed quiet a moment. "Then

turn around and I'll tell the sheriff that I want to go with you. I want to do this."

Now it was his turn to stay quiet a moment. "I don't have the hacking skills to do what needed to be done, and I didn't have the time to learn them. So, I had to hire someone." It burned Jake's throat to say this. "Someone I'm not sure I can trust."

Her dark brown eyes widened, and she apparently could guess where this was going. "Someone who might tell Tanner?"

"Yeah." And he wished he had rehearsed this part. "Ernest Garfield's son, Wade."

She cursed. "Well, heck, yes. He'll sell the information to Tanner. He'd sell his mother's eyeballs for a quarter. Why in blue blazes would you go to him, to anyone who could be paid off?"

"Because I ran out of options, that's why. And Sunny's running out of time. If she doesn't get the marrow soon, it could be too late. Right now, she's so weak that even a cold could turn out to be fatal. Every moment is a risk for her." Mercy, it hurt to say that aloud or to even think it.

"Wade said it wouldn't be long before the marshals or FBI could trace the hack job to a computer. *My* computer," he clarified. "I didn't want to implicate anyone else in this."

Her breath was gusting now, and the lip chewing got worse. "So, the marshals know what you've done, and they've probably called Coopersville's sheriff."

"Probably." And once the sheriff realized Maggie wasn't at the diner, they'd do a search. One that would include putting out an APB.

She didn't say anything. Maggie just sat there, and even though Jake hadn't thought it possible, she had even less color in her face now than when she'd dropped that coffeepot.

Maggie started to shake her head.

Jake ignored it. He wasn't taking no for an answer.

"First, you'll need a simple blood test to determine if you're a bone marrow match. If you are," he went on, "there's a procedure where the doctor extracts the marrow with a needle. It'll require some sedation, but it should all be a done deal in a day or two. I'll keep you hidden. I'll protect you as best I can. And then I can call the marshals, turn myself in and you can go back into the program under a new identity," he added. "I'm sorry about that."

Another new life. And she was no doubt thinking of the problems that would cause for her. Leaving everything behind again. Starting from scratch again.

Clearly, she had a life there in Coopersville. Not what some would consider a good life, but maybe she'd been happy. The cook at the diner had certainly looked protective of her.

Or something.

It was the same for the geezer eating the eggs. For a second, Jake had thought he might have to shoot his way out of there.

But then Maggie had stepped up and settled the situation.

Jake wanted to hang on to his hatred for her, but she'd put a dent in his hard feelings by not only offering herself to a man she considered dangerous—*him*—but also going along with this plan that could ultimately get her killed.

"I'm sorry about putting you in danger, too," he added. "I know this could get you killed. If there'd been another way, I wouldn't have done this to you."

"Yes." Maggie said it almost idly, as if she weren't really listening to him.

"Is there someone you need to call to let him know you're alive and well?" Jake asked.

"No." And she shook her head again. "No one there knows who I am. *Was,*" she corrected.

Good move. It was probably why she was still alive.

"But they'll know now," she added.

Maggie stared out the window, watching the rural landscape zip past the window. Soon he'd need to get off this road and onto another one. Then, another. It'd be all back roads to get her to Mustang Ridge.

He wondered if the marshals or the FBI would set up roadblocks. Or use helicopters to locate them. And while he was wondering, Jake thought about how his family would be taking all of this.

Royce was no doubt trying to cover his butt. Nell would be trying to keep everybody calm and make sure Sunny was okay. Chet would be pitching a fit that Jake hadn't told him what was going on. It'd be minor compared to the fit Chet had pitched two and a half years ago when he'd walked in on Jake kissing Maggie by the barn.

A kiss to soothe his pain, Jake had tried to justify, since he was grieving his wife's death.

Jake had pitched his own fit just a few hours later when he'd learned that Anna's killer was none other than Bruce Tanner and not some armed robber as everyone had thought.

And the real kicker?

Tanner had done that because he'd warned Maggie to back off an investigation she was honchoing. Of course, Maggie hadn't bothered to share that threat with the family or her sister. If she had, Jake maybe could have figured out that Tanner would go after someone Maggie loved.

He heard her phone ring, and she rifled through her purse to find it. "My boss," she relayed to Jake, but she didn't answer it.

"He's worried about you," Jake commented. "Will he

try to follow us?" In other words, how much did this guy care for Maggie? Would he go to the ends of the earth to find her?

And why did that bother Jake?

He mentally cursed. He didn't care a flying fig about Maggie's love life.

"I'll call him later," she answered. "Could you stop the truck a minute? I have to throw up."

Jake knew how she felt. That's the reaction he'd had when he first learned Sunny was sick. Plus, she was no doubt reliving all the mess with Anna and Tanner just as he was.

He glanced behind them first. No sign of the cruiser. No sign of anyone, so he eased the truck to a stop on the gravel shoulder.

Maggie stepped out, with her back to him, and looped her purse over her shoulder. "I'm sorry," she said.

Jake groaned. This better not turn into a conversation about Anna. A conversation meant to relieve Maggie of the guilt that he wanted her to have for the rest of her life.

She damn sure deserved the guilt.

So did he.

And Jake was about to remind her of just that when she slammed the truck door and jumped over the ditch.

Maggie started running toward the woods.

Chapter Four

Maggie ran as if Jake's life depended on it. Because it did. He no doubt knew that he'd opened a Texas-size can of worms by coming to her, but he had no idea just how dangerous this could be for him. For Sunny.

For his entire family.

She wouldn't be responsible for another McCall murder. *No.* This ended now.

The ground was frozen, slicked with a mixture of ice, fallen trees and dead leaves, and her sensible work shoes were ideal for standing on linoleum but not so good for navigating the slippery terrain. Still, Maggie ran and prayed that she'd gotten enough of a head start on Jake that she could disappear into the thick woods before he could catch up.

Of course, disappearing was just for starters. She'd have to hide, and she figured Jake would look for her as long as he could—maybe until the Coopersville sheriff or someone else drove by.

Maybe that wouldn't take too long.

The cold had already started to clog her lungs, but she kept fighting for each step. A thick cluster of trees was just ahead. Beyond that, the actual woods. She had no idea where those woods led; that was something else she'd have to work out.

Maggie heard the footsteps behind her. Heard Jake's profanity, too.

"Damn it, Maggie. Stop!" he called out.

She didn't. Maggie kept running and was within a few feet of that tree cluster when Jake grasped on to her shoulder. The fierce jerk he gave her had her flying right into him. Her back collided with his chest, and he hooked his left arm around her waist to anchor her in place.

Maggie fought him. He might be bigger and stronger than she was, but she had a huge reason to get away from him. She rammed her elbow into his stomach and tried to bolt. She might as well have elbowed a brick wall, and the pain shot through her funny bone.

"Why the hell are you doing this?" he snarled. "I need you to help Sunny."

"I am helping her," she managed to say.

Jake clearly didn't believe that because he cursed again and didn't let go of her. Despite the pain, she tried to elbow him again. Jake dodged that blow, put her in a bear hug and shoved her against one of the trees. In the same motion, he whirled her around to face him.

Really face him.

As in they were plastered against each other, and his eyes, nose and mouth were only an inch or two from hers. They were both breathing hard, and she took in his breath. It was almost like tasting him.

Kissing him.

And he must have realized that because he moved back a little. Just enough so she could see the fire and confusion in his eyes.

"Why?" he demanded though teeth clenched so tight that she was surprised they didn't chip.

Maggie considered how much she should say. The truth might work if it didn't cause him to wring her neck. Or somehow try to get to Tanner. Since Jake was already in a blind rage, Maggie went with a partial explanation.

"I'll go to a hospital *alone* and do the test. If I'm a match, I'll donate the bone marrow immediately, but you can't be involved in it. You can't be involved with me," she corrected.

Jake glared at her. "I don't want to get *involved* with you," he informed her. And he stepped back a little more. Probably because he realized their body parts were aligned in a nearly intimate way.

"But you will help Sunny," he added.

"Of course." Maggie had to pause, clear her throat, because it was obvious that Jake wasn't just going to accept her offer to do this alone.

But he would after she told him everything she'd done. He'd hate her more, too, but that couldn't be helped. It would save him.

She hoped.

"After Tanner was arrested for Anna's murder," she started, but had to stop and take another breath. "I went to him and cut a deal. I had evidence against his son, David, and I told Tanner I would hide it if he'd leave you and your family alone."

Without taking his glare off her, Jake stepped back even farther. "What kind of evidence?"

"The kind that would send David to jail for at least twenty years." Without Jake's body heat, she started to shiver. "Yes, I know what I did was illegal, but I had to do something to stop Tanner from killing anyone else."

"And you believed this would stop Tanner?" Jake fired back at her.

"It did stop him. Since I've been gone, he hasn't paid someone to threaten you or your family, has he?" She prayed the answer to that was no.

Jake confirmed that a few seconds later by shaking his head. "Where's the evidence?"

"Someplace safe." In fact, several places, since she'd made duplicate copies and put them in deposit boxes at three different banks.

He glanced away, only to have his gaze slash back to her. "What does this have to do with you running from me?"

Maggie tried to get control of her shivering but failed. "Tanner had his own concessions with the deal. He said if I had any association with Sunny or the rest of you, that I'd 'be sorry again.' His exact words."

And that could only mean one thing—murdering another McCall.

Jake cursed, turned as if about to storm back to the truck, but Maggie stopped him. "You can't go after him or tell anyone I have the evidence against David," she insisted. "That would give Tanner an excuse to have his henchmen gun you down."

That didn't soothe the dangerous look in his eyes.

"Think of Sunny," she reminded him.

"I am!" he practically yelled. "That's why I'm here. That's why I broke the law and put your life in danger." He cursed again and groaned. "But now you're telling me that just my association with you could get us all killed."

Maggie settled for a nod. "That's why I need to do the bone marrow test alone, and you need to go back to Mustang Ridge. You can tell your family you didn't find me, and I'll make sure the word gets to Tanner that I haven't set eyes on you."

Jake stayed quiet a moment, and the only sounds were their heavy breaths and the wind slapping at them and the bare tree branches. "What if it's already too late?" he finally asked. "What if Wade's told Tanner that I hacked into the files?"

"It's not too late." Maggie hoped. "All that Wade can tell Tanner is that you hired him. Wade doesn't know you found me." But then she stopped. "Unless you told your family."

Jake shook his head. "They don't know that I was coming here."

"You didn't even tell Royce?" His brother, and a deputy sheriff. Jake and Royce were close, and she couldn't imagine Jake keeping this from him.

"Royce knows I'm looking. He doesn't know I found you. I didn't want him involved."

Yes, she could see why. It was very possible that this would lead to Jake's arrest. He'd risked so much by finding her, but Maggie couldn't let him risk his life.

Or Sunny's.

Her phone rang again, and Maggie looked into her purse at the screen. It was her boss, Gene. Again. And she figured he'd continue to call until she answered. Worse, he might alert the Coopersville sheriff more than he was already alerted. If that was possible. She'd have to call Gene first chance she got.

Jake stayed quiet a moment. "Something's not adding up. Tanner has to know if he hurts Sunny that you'd spill the evidence you have about David." He paused, stared at her. "You would spill, wouldn't you?"

"Yes." She said it slowly, but there was no hesitation. Not about Sunny anyway. It sickened her, though, to think of Tanner harming that child.

"I obtained the evidence illegally," she admitted. And she looked at him, daring him to challenge that since he'd just done the same darn thing to find her. "If I break the pact with Tanner, he could decide that his bottom-line threat to me is more important than the risk to his son."

"Especially if Tanner can get the evidence thrown out because it was illegally obtained," Jake concluded. He added a groan. "Not much of a pact if you ask me."

"It was all I had, and I hoped if I stayed away, if I did as Tanner wanted, then it would be enough."

Jake didn't respond to that right away. "What about the Coopersville sheriff?" he asked. "And the people in the Tip Top Diner? One of them could say something that would get back to Tanner."

"I'll do some damage control." How, exactly she didn't know, but Maggie would find a way to convince them to stay quiet about what they'd seen. Maybe a boatload of lies would work.

Jake glanced around the woods and then at her. "Come on. You can't stay out in this cold, and I can drive you to your car."

"Too risky." Her car and apartment were just a block from the diner. "There's a town, Howard's Creek, not too far from here. You can drop me off at the town's edge, and I'll catch the bus into Sweetwater. I can go to the nearest hospital, have the test done and they can fax the result to Mustang Ridge. I'll use an alias in case Tanner manages to buy off someone at the hospital."

Jake stood there, apparently processing everything but not moving.

"I swear I'll do the test," she said. "I love Sunny, and I'll do whatever's necessary to help her get better."

That seemed to be the assurance he was waiting for, because Jake gave her a nod, turned and started for the truck. Maggie let out the breath she'd been holding, and she hurried to catch up with him.

"On the bus ride to Sweetwater, I'll call my boss at the

diner," she added, more for herself than for him, "and I'll tell him you're someone I met in a bar last weekend. I can give him enough details to ease his suspicions."

And maybe, just maybe, Jake's visit wouldn't undo the deal she'd made with Tanner and set off the powder keg Maggie had been sitting on for two and a half years. Of course, Jake was sitting on a powder keg of a different sort.

After that, she'd need to ditch the phone in case the marshals tried to use it to try to track her. The phone had special security measures on it, to prevent just anyone from finding her, but right now, the marshals were a concern. If they found her, they found Jake.

"How sick is Sunny?" she asked.

Jake didn't stop walking, didn't look back, but she saw his shoulders tense. "I told you it was bad, and it is. She's very sick and won't get better without a transplant."

That cut through her hard. Mercy, this was so unfair. Her little niece had already been through too much. Jake, as well. And Maggie prayed she could help in all of this. Not that it would absolve her of any guilt in Anna's death.

No.

Nothing could ever do that, but at least she had the chance to save Jake from having to lose someone else he loved.

"I'll be arrested soon," he said, still not looking back as they walked to the truck. "But Royce can handle the test results. He'll see to things."

The words had barely left his mouth when Jake came to an abrupt stop, and Maggie nearly plowed right into him. He lifted his head and appeared to listen for something. Maggie did the same, but she heard nothing.

"Move, now!" Jake insisted, and he caught her arm.

Maggie hadn't exactly been at ease, but that gave her another jab of fear and concern. Jake started to run with her in tow, but they were still a good twenty feet from the truck when she finally heard something.

Something Maggie didn't want to hear.

A gunshot.

JAKE HOOKED HIS ARM around Maggie and dragged her to the ground.

It wasn't a second too soon because the second shot came almost immediately after the first, and both slammed into the ground right where they'd been standing. There weren't many places he could use for cover so he pulled her behind a fallen tree. It wouldn't give them much protection, but it might be enough if he could pinpoint the shooter.

Jake drew his gun.

He followed the direction of the third shot. It hadn't come from the road or even near his truck but instead had come from the right, and his attention zoomed in on a group of cottonwood trees. It wasn't deep cover, but it was just enough for a gunman to hide.

Tanner's hired gunman, no doubt.

If Coopersville's sheriff had found Maggie and him, the lawman wouldn't have shot first, especially since Maggie could have been hurt. Unless Tanner had already managed to get the sheriff on his payroll.

The next shot smacked into the fallen tree and sent some splinters and bark flying through the air. Jake pulled Maggie lower, until she was flat on the ground, and he covered her body with his. He couldn't risk her being shot and killed, because she was the only one who could save Sunny.

He'd die for her, if necessary.

Ironic, since more often than not, he'd been the one to want her dead. Or at least he'd wanted her grieving at much as he was.

"If it's Tanner's man, I can negotiate with him," she insisted.

"This isn't a negotiating situation." And the next round of bullets hopefully proved that to her. Jake took aim at the cottonwoods and fired a shot of his own. Not that he had the shooter in line of sight, but he didn't want this guy moving in closer for an easier kill.

"I still have that proof to send David to jail," she reminded Jake.

Yeah. But that apparently wasn't stopping Tanner. Of course, maybe the man just had plans to kill Jake. That would take care of his threat to make Maggie "sorry again," but Tanner could still use threat of violence against the rest of the McCalls to keep Maggie from turning over that evidence to the authorities.

"Tanner wants me," Jake relayed to her. "If that happens, get the hell out of here and go to the hospital in Sweetwater. Don't waste any time reporting any of this."

Even over the sound of the next shot, Jake heard Maggie curse. "You're not going to sacrifice yourself."

"Might not have a choice. Time's running out."

Her cursing got significantly worse. "Do you have a backup weapon?"

But she didn't wait for him to answer. Maggie must have remembered that he wore a boot holster because she scrambled lower so she could jerk up his jeans' leg and retrieve the small Beretta.

"It's me, Maggie Gallagher," she shouted. "And you can tell your worthless spit wad of a boss that if I die, the evidence against his son will automatically go to a dozen different law enforcement agencies. David Tanner will rot in jail."

She fired a shot into the trees to punctuate that, but it didn't stop the bullets from coming at them.

Hell.

Maybe he'd been wrong about this being Tanner's man. Or maybe Tanner wasn't going to give in to Maggie's threat. Of course, the gunman could just be stupid, and if so, he might end up killing them both.

Enough of this.

"Stay down," Jake warned Maggie, and he lifted himself up a little so he could actually see into the trees. It took him a few seconds to locate the silhouette of the shooter who was dressed in camouflage.

It took Jake another second to aim.

Jake double tapped the trigger and sent the two bullets into the man. There was no groan of pain, just the sickening thuds of the shots slamming into the body.

He saw the man drop to the ground, but Jake didn't waste any time. He took Maggie's arm again, dragging her from the ground, and he started running toward the truck. She kept the Beretta aimed in the direction of the fallen man, but Jake figured the guy was incapable of returning fire.

Of course, he could have a partner.

Or two.

And that's why Jake ran as fast as he could. Sunny didn't have time for Maggie and him to fight off any other hired guns.

Since the passenger's side door was still wide-open, Jake dove in, scrambling across the seat, and he pulled Maggie in with him. The engine was running, just as he'd left it, and he didn't wait for her to close the door. He threw the truck into gear, and he hit the accelerator.

Maggie slammed the door and turned in the seat so she could watch behind them. She was the cop now, and even though that brought back bad memories of her investigation that had gotten Anna killed, he wouldn't refuse having her as backup.

Temporary backup, that is.

The plan was still to get her to Sweetwater, but first he had to call Royce and warn him. Nothing would stop Jake from getting into the prison and tearing Tanner limb from limb if the man had already sent his hired guns to the ranch.

Jake took out his phone while he volleyed his attention between the side mirror and the road ahead. There was no sign of the sheriff's cruiser. No sign of a gunman, either, so maybe that meant they could actually make it out of there without having to dodge any more bullets.

He pressed in Royce's number, and his brother answered on the first ring. "Where the hell are you?" Royce demanded.

Jake ignored that question. "You need to secure the ranch. Tanner could have men on the way out there."

His brother said something that Jake didn't catch. "I'll call you right back." And Royce hung up.

Jake prayed his brother could put enough security measures in place to keep Sunny safe, and he cursed Maggie and himself for the deal that she'd made with Tanner. The deal might have kept them safe for the past two and a half years, but now it could get them killed. He should have anticipated something like this. Nothing was ever easy when it came to dealing with Tanner.

Or Maggie.

"Wade must have spilled his guts to Tanner or David right away," Maggie mumbled. She was still keeping watch behind them.

Yeah, that was possible, because Tanner and his son still had a boatload of money, and even with Tanner behind bars, that didn't mean the father and son criminal duo couldn't hire all the guns and muscle they needed.

Guns and muscle that could be aimed at Sunny.

"Tanner doesn't want to hurt Sunny," Maggie said, as if reading his mind. But it sure sounded as if she was trying to convince herself. "You're the one he'll go after."

"Sunny is your niece," he reminded her. Hell, he wished he could transport himself back to the ranch so he could protect his baby.

"There's something else that might be playing into this," she said. "Tanner knows about that kiss in the barn."

Jake's left hand tightened on the steering wheel. "How the hell would he have known about that?"

"I'm not sure. I think your father said something, and it got around town. All I know is that Tanner brought it up when I went to talk to him about that deal." Maggie paused. "He thinks you have feelings for me and vice versa."

Well, Tanner was wrong about that. "Surely, he knows the truth by now?"

"Maybe not. Maybe he thinks your talk of hating me is to cover up the feelings that went behind that kiss."

"It's not a cover," Jake snapped. And the kiss hadn't been about feelings. It'd been about his stupid clouded judgment because he'd lost his wife just a couple of months earlier.

Months that Maggie hadn't volunteered that she had been the reason Anna was killed. There was a chance she hadn't known that exact information at the time, but she sure as heck could have told Jake about the investigation she'd started against Tanner. Two months was a long time to conceal that information.

The moment his phone buzzed, he glanced at the screen, saw his brother's number, and he pressed the answer button.

"I alerted all the ranch hands. Nell and Dad, too," Royce said. "Everyone is armed, but how soon can you get back?"

Jake glanced at Maggie and at the Colt that he still had gripped in his hand. He needed to get her to a doctor or a hospital for that test, but he couldn't do that with his little girl at risk.

"I'll hurry," Jake answered, "but I'm still about three hours out."

"Get back as fast as you can. Nell said Sunny was upset when she saw her granddaddy running to get his gun."

Hell. The image of that was too vivid in his head, and Jake automatically sped up.

"Take the back road to get to the ranch," Royce added. "And keep a low profile once you're—"

"Maggie's with me," Jake interrupted. He glanced at her again, and she was clearly waiting to hear what was going on back in Mustang Ridge.

Royce didn't answer right away. "I'll let Dad know she's coming, too."

Jake could hear the dread in Royce's tone. That same dread went through Jake. This would not be a pleasant homecoming for any of them, especially Maggie.

"I'll remind Dad that Maggie came to help," Royce said. "She did come to help, right?"

Jake settled for a "Yeah."

"One more thing," Jake added. "A gunman fired shots at Maggie and me in the woods east of Coopersville. I had to leave a dead body behind, but you need to figure out a way to get someone out there to investigate."

Royce cursed again. "I'll turn it in as an anonymous tip, but if it was Tanner's doing, he'll probably have already arranged for his own cleanup."

That was fine with Jake. One less thing on his plate, but he wouldn't mind someone other than Tanner's henchmen checking the body for any evidence to prove who'd hired him.

"I'll see you when I get back," Jake told Royce.

"Wait. There's something else. Like I said, use the back roads, and whatever you do, don't come into town."

"Why?" Jake asked cautiously.

"The U.S. marshals showed up about fifteen minutes ago. I've talked them out of going to the ranch because of Sunny's illness. I swore to them I'd get you to come here to the sheriff's office instead."

Royce paused, a long time. "Jake, they're here to arrest you."

Chapter Five

Maggie had so many bad feelings about going to the McCall ranch, but none of those could override the fact that Jake had no choice in the matter. He couldn't risk Tanner coming after Sunny. He needed to be there at home with his daughter in case there was an attack.

And that meant Maggie would be there, too.

She'd taken as many precautions as she could. She had made a call to her boss, Gene, to try to convince him that she was all right. And that she'd be back in a day or two. That was an outright lie. She couldn't go back to Coopersville, and within seconds of telling Gene that lie, Maggie had ended the call, disassembled her phone and tossed the parts out the window.

Now, she kept watch out the side mirror as Jake snaked the truck over the familiar farm roads that led to the ranch. Maggie recognized every part of the scenery, since she'd been born and raised in Mustang Ridge. She also had no trouble recalling from memory all the details of the McCall ranch.

Or the threat that Chet had made the day she left.

Something about killing her and the horse she rode in on if she ever returned. Maggie didn't think that colorful threat was all bluff, either, but maybe Chet could put his hatred aside long enough for her to get this test done.

Jake finished his call to Royce, the fourth on their nearly three hour drive from Coopersville, and he slipped the phone into his pocket. "Dr. Grange will come out to the ranch to do the bone marrow test on you," he relayed to her.

Maggie silently groaned. "Tanner can buy off the doctor." But the same was true for just about anyone.

Jake made a weary sound of agreement. "Royce told Doc Grange that he needed to check on Sunny. He doesn't know you'll be at the ranch."

Well, that was a start, but Grange would soon know that it was a lie. Somehow she had to convince him to keep her return a secret. After convincing the doctor, she'd have to get in touch with Tanner and remind him of their agreement. An agreement that had been broken because she was back in Mustang Ridge.

But maybe she could keep that from him.

Jake took the final turn onto one of the ranch trails. Winter was hardly the best time to be sloshing through the icy dirt paths, but this was one more step in keeping her arrival a secret. They passed the outbuildings. Barns.

Including *the* barn of the infamous kiss.

She glanced at Jake, but he was looking everywhere but there, which only seemed to call more attention to it.

Maggie spotted several ranch hands, all armed, and there was another in the backyard where Jake finally brought the truck to a stop. He'd barely had time to kill the engine when the door opened and his sister, Nell, stepped out. Once, Maggie and she had been friends. Judging from Nell's troubled eyes, Maggie wasn't expecting that friendship to resume.

It was understandable.

Nell had been friends with Anna. In fact, they weren't just in-laws; they'd worked together at the county clerk's office in town.

"Is she a match?" Nell asked the moment Jake opened the door.

"We'll soon find out. That's why the doc is on the way." He motioned for Maggie to come across the seat on his side. Probably so she wouldn't be out in the open any longer than necessary, and he quickly ushered her inside.

Nell held the door open for them and studied Maggie's uniform and then her muddy shoes. "I'm guessing you had a rough morning, too."

Maggie nodded. It'd been nearly three years of rough mornings.

The kitchen was toasty warm and smelled liked Christmas cookies. Leave it to Nell to bake cookies when all hell was breaking loose, but then that's what Maggie had always admired about her cool-under-pressure former friend.

Nothing had changed much in the time she'd been gone. The place looked exactly as it had when Anna and she had started visiting as teenagers. In those days, they'd both had crushes on Jake.

Something that would be a good idea to forget.

Like the house, Nell hadn't changed much, either, though Maggie thought she was looking more and more like her late mother. In fact, she was pretty sure she'd seen Mrs. McCall wear that very apron. The cross necklace and the engagement ring, too, though Nell was wearing the ring on her right hand instead of her left.

"I'm sorry about your mother's death," Maggie told her. Breast cancer, Jake had told her when she'd asked on the drive over.

Nell nodded. "It was a tough loss for Jake, Royce and me." She didn't add her father to that list, and Maggie knew why. Even though they stayed married, Nell's parents had had a rocky relationship.

"I went ahead and sent Betsy home," Nell told Jake. She

put on the oven mitt and took out another baking sheet of cookies from the oven. "I didn't figure it'd be a good idea if she was here, what with possible trouble brewing."

"You're right." Jake glanced at Maggie. "Betsy Becker, the nurse who's been taking care of Sunny."

Oh, *that* Betsy. Maggie remembered the kindly woman, and Nell had been right to get her away from this. The fewer people, the better.

"You have a security system?" Maggie asked, looking at the windows and then the door.

Jake nodded. "And the ranch hands are watching both roads."

Maybe that would be enough. *Maybe.* But the Tanners had a long reach when it came to settling a score.

Nell turned to her brother. "Why would Tanner try to come after us now? And why are those marshals waiting at your office to arrest you?"

That last part snagged Maggie's attention. "What marshals?"

"The ones who arrived several hours ago," Nell clarified.

"You knew about this?" Maggie asked him, but there was no answer required. She could tell from his expression that he knew. The marshals obviously hadn't had any trouble tracing the hacking job back to Jake.

"Well?" Nell pressed.

Jake shrugged. "It's a long story."

"Shorten it," Nell insisted, staring at Maggie now.

Since the cat was out of the proverbial bag, Maggie didn't see a reason to keep it secret. "Jake hacked into the classified database to find me."

"Mercy," Nell mumbled. "Is that why the ranch hands are all armed—to keep the marshals away?"

"No. Royce is supposed to keep the marshals away." Jake tipped his head to Maggie for her to finish.

"I made a deal with Tanner so he'd leave all of you alone. He might believe I broke that deal." She lifted her shoulder. "Technically, I did."

"What did Tanner threaten to do if you broke the deal?" Nell asked.

"To hurt one or more of you." She had to pause. "I have evidence against his son, so that might be enough to tie Tanner's hands." Another pause. "Unless he thinks he can have the evidence negated in some way."

Or maybe Tanner would let his temper get the best of him and lash out despite the consequences.

"The idea is to get Maggie out of here fast and back into WITSEC," Jake explained. "Then, I can deal with the marshals."

Nell practically slammed the cookies onto the counter. "And you'll be off to jail."

Jake nodded. "I did what I had to do."

Tears sprang to Nell's eyes. "I know." And she repeated it as she gave his arm a gentle squeeze.

"I had no choice but to bring her here," Maggie heard Jake say.

Maggie's attention shifted to the doorway where she spotted Chet approaching them. Definitely no warm fuzzies from him. He gave her a withering look, cursed and walked away.

"I can go as soon as the test is done," Maggie assured Jake and Nell. She cleared her throat. "But I'd like to see Sunny first."

Maggie braced herself for a resounding no from both of them, but they exchanged glances. There was some sibling telepathy going on between them, because Nell lifted her left eyebrow. Waited. Jake waited, too, and then finally echoed the profanity his father had just used.

"Wash your hands," Jake ordered. "Scrub them clean and take one of the masks." He pointed to a dispenser box of surgical masks on the windowsill next to the clay pots of fresh herbs.

For fear he would change his mind, Maggie didn't waste any time. She shucked off her coat, which Nell took, and Maggie hurried to the sink. Jake did as well, and they both reached for the bottle of antibacterial soap. His hand brushed against hers, causing him to jerk back, but they kept scrubbing until Maggie was certain she couldn't get any cleaner.

"This way," Jake growled. He took two masks and handed her one. "Keep it short, and don't you dare say a word about Anna. I'll be the one to explain it."

Maggie nodded and gave Nell a silent thanks for urging this, and she followed Jake out of the kitchen, through the great room and to the doorway of the guest suite. Now, here was a room that had changed. It was crammed with Christmas decorations and toys. The bed was the only part of the original furniture that remained, and Sunny was there, in the center of that bed.

Maggie's heart went to her knees.

Oh, God.

She hadn't expected the emotion to slam into her like this. Or the tears. She blinked them back, but she doubted she could keep them at bay for long. Anna's little baby wasn't so little anymore. A proper little girl dressed in a frilly pink gown and with those dark brown curls haloing around her face.

She looked sick and weak, but when she saw Maggie in the doorway, Sunny smiled. It was more than a smile. Her face lit up brighter than the lights on the nearby Christmas tree.

"Are you my mommy?" Sunny asked. She lifted a weak hand to the picture on the nightstand next to her. It was a shot of Anna holding Sunny when she was a baby. "Did the angels bring you back?"

Because her legs didn't feel any steadier than her stomach, Maggie held on to the door frame. "No," she managed to say. She looked at Jake, shook her head. She had no idea how to answer that. She certainly hadn't anticipated that Sunny would think she was Anna.

"It's not Mommy." Jake's voice was shakier than Maggie's. "Royce said you were upset earlier," he continued, changing the subject. He put on his mask, moved Maggie aside and went to his daughter. He kissed her forehead and sank down on the bed next to her.

Sunny nodded. "'Cause you weren't here to give me a morning kiss. Or read to me. And I saw Grandpa with his gun. I didn't like that." She pulled him down for a hug. "Where were you, Daddy?"

Even though Sunny was clearly upset, each word seemed precious to Maggie. Like a gift she'd never thought she could have. Before seeing Sunny, she'd already made up her mind to do whatever it took to help her, but now Maggie was even more determined.

"I had to do some things," Jake assured the little girl, "but I'm here now. And I brought your aunt Maggie to meet you."

Sunny looked at Maggie, and the smile returned though her head did ease back down onto the pillow. "My aunt Maggie? Like Aunt Nell?"

Jake nodded. "Except Nell is my sister, and Maggie is your mommy's sister. That's why they look alike."

Sunny frowned. "So, the angels didn't bring Mommy back for Christmas?"

"No." Jake swallowed hard. "Remember, we talked about this? Mommy can't come back. She has to live with the angels."

Sunny looked over her dad's shoulder at Maggie. "So maybe the angels sent me Aunt Maggie instead?"

"Maybe," Jake answered.

Sunny managed another weak smile and motioned toward the book next to the picture on the nightstand. "Then, maybe Aunt Maggie can read to me." She looked at her dad perhaps for approval and must have seen the surprise, or maybe even the disgust for Maggie, in his eyes. "Just this one day," Sunny added. "Daddy, you can read to me tomorrow."

When Sunny continued to glance at the book, Maggie put on the mask, went closer and picked it up. She wasn't sure what Jake was going to do and was more than a little surprised when he moved off the edge of the bed to make room for her. He'd no sooner done that when his phone buzzed.

"I have to take this call," he said, looking down at the screen. Then, he shot Maggie a warning glance. "Remember what I said."

Yes, no mention of Anna. Maggie had no intentions of violating that rule. She waited until Jake had stepped out before she sat on the bed next to Sunny. She opened the first page of the book about baby animals, but Sunny put her hand over Maggie's.

"It's okay," she whispered like a secret. "I know how to read it myself. Some of the words anyway."

"Then you must be very smart," Maggie answered.

Sunny gave a shrug that reminded Maggie so much of Jake. In fact, her niece was more McCall than Gallagher.

"You know I'm sick?" Sunny asked.

Maggie nodded, and she tried to push back the tears again. "But you'll get better."

Another shrug, and Sunny looked up at her with those big blue-gray eyes that were a genetic copy of Jake's. "Did the angels send you 'cause I'm sick?"

"I wanted to see you," Maggie settled for saying. Best not to mention the bone marrow test since she might not even be a match. That broke Maggie's heart just to think of the possibility.

"Daddy said Mommy lives with the angels. They take care of Mommy now."

Maggie didn't trust her voice and just nodded.

Sunny motioned toward the angel ornaments on the tree. "They take care of me, too." Her voice was weak, and her eyelids drifted down for a moment. "I get tired a lot."

Since there was no answer to that, Maggie settled for pushing away a curl that had dropped down onto Sunny's cheek. Like the words Sunny had spoken, that simple touch was precious, too.

"Know what I want for Christmas?" Sunny asked. "I want you to live with me and be my mommy."

Maggie nearly choked on the quick breath she sucked in, and her reaction didn't improve when she heard the sound behind her. Maggie looked over her shoulder and saw Jake standing in the doorway. He'd obviously finished his call. He'd also heard what his daughter had just said.

"I need to speak to your aunt," he told Sunny. Because his mask was off, Maggie could see that his jaw was tight again. Teeth semiclenched, too.

Despite the glare Jake shot her, Maggie kissed Sunny's forehead. "Sleep tight, sweetheart."

Maggie put the book back on the nightstand before she

joined Jake outside the room. He shut the door and looked down at her as if waiting for an explanation.

"I didn't bring up Anna." Maggie pulled off her mask. "And that last part she said—that was all Sunny's idea. I had nothing to do with it."

His glare stayed in place for several seconds before he muttered some profanity. "I didn't hear what she said. Why don't you tell me?"

Oh. She'd thought from his sour expression that he'd been reacting to Sunny's mommy wish, but maybe the mood hadn't been for anything specifically said, just for the fact that Maggie was there.

"Thank you for letting me see her," Maggie told him.

She braced herself for some kind of verbal blast, because she figured Jake was kicking himself for allowing the little visit. Chet was certainly adding to that mental kicking because he was standing in the great room with yet another McCall glare aimed at her.

However, he wasn't alone.

Maggie recognized the man next to Jake's father. It was Dr. Gavin Grange, and after studying his body language, she wondered if at least part of Chet's glare wasn't meant for the doctor and not just her.

"Dr. Grange will do the blood test now," Jake informed her.

She volleyed glances among the three. "Is there a problem I don't know about?"

"The doc's just worried about his own hide," Chet snarled.

Dr. Grange didn't confirm that. Not with words anyway. But he came closer, set his medical bag on the table in the entry and extracted a syringe with a needle.

Maggie held out her arm for the doctor to wipe the spot with an antiseptic pad. She winced a little when he shoved the needle into her vein, and he drew not one but two vials of blood. He put the blood vials in his medical bag.

"How soon before we know the results?" she asked.

"I'll ask the lab to expedite it."

"Stay on them," Chet piped in. "I want those results today."

That caused the doctor to scowl, and he gathered his things before he turned to Jake. "I can't make it happen that soon. Usually, an expedited test still has a twenty-four-hour turnaround, and the hospital lab is closing early today because tomorrow's Christmas Eve."

Maggie groaned softly. The holidays would slow things to a crawl, and the weather wouldn't help, either. It was ironic, because normally a white Christmas would have been a perfect way to celebrate, but it would only be perfect if they could get those test results and learn that she was a match.

"If you could speed that up, I'd appreciate it," Jake told him.

The doctor nodded. "If Maggie's a match, I won't be able to do the marrow harvesting. You'll have to take her to Amarillo for that so you might want to go ahead and make arrangements in case you get lucky with the match."

Maggie wondered if that's because it was beyond his medical expertise or if it was because he didn't want to be involved further in this.

"Call me the second you have the results," Jake insisted at the same moment Chet told the doctor, "You can see yourself out."

The doctor did just that. He headed for the door and didn't look back.

"What's wrong with him?" Maggie asked.

"You," Chet quickly provided. "And me. He didn't want

to get involved because of what happened with Anna, but I convinced him otherwise."

"How?" And Maggie was afraid to hear the answer.

"I reminded him of how many people in this town I could bad-mouth him to," Chet explained. "Then, I told him he'd be damn sorry if he didn't keep all of this secret. If it leaks out that you're here in Mustang Ridge, I'm putting the blame on him."

Well, that explained Grange's uneasy attitude. Still, in this case she was glad for the threat, especially if it would get them those test results any faster.

"What now?" Maggie asked Jake.

"We wait."

Under normal circumstances, that wouldn't have been such a bad thing since she might have another opportunity to spend time with her niece, but this was far from normal.

Jake cracked Sunny's door a little and looked in on her. Maggie did, too, but Sunny was sound asleep. Neither of them moved. They both stood there, staring in at her.

Maggie wanted to say so many things. How sorry she was that her sister wasn't there to be with this precious child. She wanted to tell Jake that he'd done a good job raising her, that Sunny was smart, beautiful and a dozen other adjectives that he wouldn't want to hear. Not from her. So, Maggie just held her peace and watched Sunny sleep.

"Thank you," Jake whispered.

It took Maggie a moment to realize he was talking to her about the bone marrow test. "You don't have to thank me. You risked a lot to get me back here."

"You risked a lot more by coming." He turned his head, stared at her. "I swear I'll do everything within my power to get you out of this alive."

That was nearly as powerful as Sunny's smile and

words. And even though she knew Jake would never forgive her, it eased the pain in her heart a little.

"And I'll do everything within my power to stop you from being arrested," Maggie promised. What exactly that would be, she didn't know, but talking to the marshals was a start.

"We don't need that kind of help from you," Chet said. Obviously, he'd eavesdropped on their conversation.

"Tough." Maggie glanced over her shoulder at him. "Because you're going to get it anyway. You can hate me all you want. But Jake needs to be here with his daughter."

Chet made a gruff, skeptical sound, and then his attention drifted lower. To the position of Jake's and her bodies. They were literally side by side. Touching. And while Jake wasn't giving her a loving look, he wasn't bristling at her, either.

The man's gaze snapped to Jake. "I don't guess I have to remind you to think with your head and not with what's behind your zipper."

That got Jake bristling. His jaw muscles stirred again, and Maggie figured he'd step away from her. He didn't.

"No," Jake said to his father, "you don't have to remind me."

Maybe it was Jake's chilly tone or the fact he hadn't budged, but Chet said something under his breath, took his gun from the mantel over the fireplace and headed toward the door. "I'm doing a walk around the place."

Maggie waited until he was out the door before she said anything else. "I don't want to cause friction between your father and you."

"You didn't." Now, he stepped away, and he went to the side windows by the front door and looked out. "There's always friction between us."

Maggie thought about that a moment. "Does Sunny get caught up in it?"

"No," he quickly assured her. He didn't have time to say more because the house phone rang.

Probably because he didn't want the ringing sound to wake up Sunny, he hurried to the foyer table, but Maggie heard Nell answer it in the kitchen. A moment later, Nell appeared in the doorway, and she had a concerned look on her face.

"It's Betsy on the phone," Nell told them. "She says she has to talk to you right away. I didn't tell her you were here in case the marshals are trying to use her to find you. I just told her I had to check a pot on the stove and put her on hold."

Betsy Becker, Sunny's nurse. Maggie hoped this wasn't bad news.

"Betsy wouldn't tell the marshals anything," Jake assured his sister. He pressed the speaker call button on the phone on the foyer table. "Betsy," he answered. "Is something wrong?"

"Could be. I got a bad feeling about this, Jake."

"About what?" he pressed.

"I stopped by the hospital for supplies after I left the ranch, and I heard some talk that David Tanner was here. And not just *here,* but he was talking to Dr. Grange right before the doc left to go out to the ranch."

Maggie groaned. She'd suspected something was wrong with the doctor, and now she knew what. God knows what David had said to the man and had perhaps threatened him.

One look at Jake, and Maggie knew he was thinking the same thing she was: Had the threat worked?

And had Dr. Grange just betrayed them?

"I have to get you out of here," Jake said. *"Fast."*

Chapter Six

The moment Jake ended the call with Betsy, he flipped open his phone and punched in Royce's number.

"What can I do to help?" Maggie frantically asked.

Judging from her tone and the renewed fear in her eyes, she knew what Betsy's warning had meant: Dr. Grange could have told Tanner that Maggie was back in Mustang Ridge. And if he had, then Tanner would know that Maggie had violated their agreement, and he'd send assassins to the ranch to try to kill her.

"Tell Nell what's going on," Jake said to her. "And see if she can find you some warmer clothes to wear. I want everyone ready to leave in a half hour or less." Which wasn't much time, of course, so he had to get moving. "Royce, Dad and Nell will take Sunny someplace safe. Someplace far away from us."

He hated the thought of being away from his little girl, but he didn't want her around if Tanner came after Maggie and him.

"Royce," Jake said, the moment that his brother answered the phone. "Are the marshals still there at the sheriff's office?"

"Yep." Since that was all he said, it probably meant the lawmen were within listening distance.

"Is it safe to talk?" Jake asked.

"It is, but make it quick. I want to keep the line open in case my brother calls."

Yeah, they were definitely listening, and Royce was trying to make them believe the call was from someone else. "I need you to come to the ranch. It's possible Dr. Grange told Tanner that Maggie was here. I have to move her. Sunny, too."

Royce stayed quiet a moment. "Did he actually hit you, Mrs. Henderson?" he asked, still playing the part for the marshals. "All right, sounds as if he's on a bender. I'll come out there and talk to him. Be there in ten minutes."

When Royce hung up, Jake called his dad's phone to tell Chet to get back to the house. The third call was to Tommy Rester, one of the ranch hands, and Jake asked the man to tighten the security around the ranch and then come to the house so he could run an errand.

"I can call the marshals," Jake heard Maggie say.

She was in the doorway between the kitchen and the great room, and she'd no doubt heard his call to Tommy.

He shook his head. "I don't want them or anyone to know you're with me. And even if you don't tell them that, they might guess."

Right now, he just wanted to focus on leaving, not the marshals.

Nell came rushing into the room, her face as harried as Jake's probably was. "I put together a food basket for Maggie and you. Some clothes, too. Where will you be going?"

"I'd rather not say, but the rest of you will be taking Sunny to the hospital in Amarillo."

Nell nodded. "I'll pack some of Sunny's things."

Jake took her by the arm. "After watching Betsy all this time, you think you could draw blood if you had to?"

His sister's mouth dropped open. "What's wrong with Sunny? Why does she need a blood test right away?"

"She doesn't. It's for Maggie. I don't want to rely on Dr. Grange to get her samples to the lab. If you can draw the blood, it'd save me from having to take her to a doctor somewhere."

Nell glanced at Maggie, who only nodded, and his sister hurried into Sunny's room. It only took her a few seconds before she came back with a needle and syringe. Jake didn't watch as Nell drew the blood. Instead, he went to the front window, and the moment he saw the ranch hand Tommy Rester step onto the porch, he opened the door for him.

"I need you to do an errand," Jake instructed. As soon as Nell had the vial of blood ready, he handed it to Tommy. "Drive this to the Amarillo P.D. crime lab and ask them to process it. I need it compared to Sunny's bone marrow, and all her information is in the national registry files. Understand?"

Tommy gave a shaky nod. The young man no doubt understood the severity of what was going on, and Jake hoped he could get the sample to Amarillo without interference. Jake figured Tanner had more important things on his mind, like some kind of revenge against Maggie, to go after a ranch hand.

"I'll get Sunny's clothes," Nell said, hurrying up the stairs.

Jake had a dozen things spinning through his mind, but he looked at Maggie to make sure she was okay. She was dabbing her arm where Nell had drawn the blood, but she was also looking at him.

"If he manages to kill me," Maggie said, her voice trembling a little, "I don't think you'd be able to use the bone marrow."

Ah, hell. He definitely didn't want Maggie thinking in that direction.

"Then, that's more reason for me to keep you alive." He

didn't bother to make that sound nice, either. He wanted Maggie fighting mad and not in this worst-case-scenario mode.

"Maybe you should just take me to the hospital now," she suggested. "And get the marrow."

It might come down to that, but for now Jake was just looking for a match. Without that match, he'd have a hard time convincing a doctor to harvest bone marrow.

The door flew open, and Jake automatically reached for his gun, but it wasn't an assassin who came through the door. It was Royce.

"I made sure the marshals didn't follow me," Royce informed them. He spared Maggie a cool glance before he looked at Jake. "The Coopersville cops didn't find a body, and they're getting hammered by a snowstorm. My guess is the search for the body will have to wait."

That was too bad, because the elements might destroy any evidence. But Jake had more important things on his hands, and the only way to prevent more people from dying was to focus on what was happening now. He certainly wasn't putting a dead assassin over Sunny's safety.

"I need Nell, Dad and you to take Sunny to the Memorial hospital in Amarillo," Jake told his brother. "Bring several ranch hands with you but keep off the main roads. And call Betsy and ask her to meet you there."

Royce didn't even blink. "How soon do we leave?"

"As soon as Nell has everything ready."

Royce nodded and tipped his head to Maggie. "What about her?"

"She's going with me, and we'll disappear until we get the test results back." Which he hoped would be *soon*. Once they were away from the ranch, he needed to start making calls to see about speeding up both sets of test results.

Royce walked closer to Maggie, snagged her gaze "Thanks for coming." He didn't wait for her to respond Royce turned and went into Sunny's room.

That was Jake's reminder that he needed to tell his little girl goodbye, and that wouldn't be easy. He wanted to be with Sunny, so he could be the one to protect her, but if he showed up at the hospital, it wouldn't take long for word to get back to the marshals.

And he'd be arrested.

He wouldn't do Sunny or Maggie much good if he was behind bars.

Jake stepped into the room and saw that Sunny was still asleep. Good. Maybe she'd stay that way for the entire drive. He held a mask over his face, went to her bed leaned down and kissed her. She opened her eyes for just a moment and smiled at him.

"I love you, baby," he whispered, but if she heard him she didn't respond.

"Ready?" Royce asked him when Jake didn't move.

Jake forced himself away from the bed, glanced back and saw Maggie in the doorway. She was still holding her arm, and there were tears in her eyes. Jake choked down his own sadness. Tears and sadness wouldn't help Sunny now, and he had to get her away from the ranch.

Royce tucked the blankets around Sunny and lifted her into his arms. He stepped out in the foyer just as Nell came down the stairs carrying a suitcase that no doubt contained some of Sunny's things.

"Just got off the phone with Dad," Nell said. "He's getting the SUV ready, and it's parked out back."

Later, Jake would need to thank his father for helping, especially for the part about not pitching a fit when Jake brought Maggie to the house. Under the circumstances, a fit wouldn't have been reasonable, but Chet didn't always operate on reason.

"I'll call you when we get to the hospital," Nell assured Jake, and they started for the back door just as Royce's phone buzzed.

Shifting Sunny in his arms, Royce took his phone from his pocket and glanced at the screen. "It's David Tanner."

Why the devil would he be calling now? Jake wanted to tell Royce to let the call go to voice mail, but maybe this was a chance to find out what David had on his mind. However, before Jake could voice that, his own phone buzzed, and he saw it was from his dad.

"Anything wrong?" Jake asked the moment he hit the answer button.

"Yeah. Just got word from one of the hands that David Tanner is at the front gate of the ranch. What does the SOB want?"

"I'm not sure, but Royce is about to find out."

Royce quickly handed Sunny to Nell, and he took the call on Speaker. Not that she needed the reminder, but Jake motioned for Maggie to stay quiet. He'd do the same because even though they were about to leave, he didn't want David blabbing to the marshals that he was there. It might get Royce in hot water.

Jake went to the front sidelight window, but he didn't step directly in front of it. He looked outside and spotted the upscale silver car and the man standing beside it.

"That's David all right," Maggie said, glancing at the window as well.

"What do you want?" Royce snapped into the phone. Definitely not a warm greeting to David.

"Good day to you, too, Royce. I'm at the front gate of the ranch, and one of your workers has a shotgun pointed at me. He insists Jake isn't there, but I believe otherwise."

"Believe what you want," Royce fired back.

"It's admirable, you covering for him, but there's no reason for that. I just want to talk to him, and trust me, what I have to say is important. It would be in his best interest, and Sunny's, to listen."

Jake's stomach knotted. He didn't want this slime to mention Sunny's name.

"Is that some kind of threat?" Royce challenged.

"Just the opposite," David insisted. "Tell Jake I need to speak to him now, and that I'll be waiting for him out here. The information I have for him could save Maggie's life." He paused a heartbeat. "And his daughter's."

MAGGIE TRIED NOT TO REACT, but the last thing David said took away some of her breath.

What the heck was this visit all about? Why include Sunny in it?

Maybe David had heard rumors that Maggie was back. Or more than rumors. If Wade had squealed to David's father about the computer hacking he did for Jake, then Tanner would have likely called his son.

"David's bluffing," Jake concluded after Royce hit the end-call button.

Probably. But Maggie figured the man knew something. Now, whether that *something* would save Sunny's and her lives was anyone's guess.

"Go ahead and get Sunny to the hospital," Jake told his siblings.

With Sunny cradled in her arms, Nell turned to leave, but Maggie leaned over and gave the child a goodbye kiss on the top of her head. She prayed she'd get to see Sunny again soon, and while she was praying, Maggie added that the marrow test would be a match.

Nell headed toward the back of the house where the

SUV was waiting to whisk them away, but Royce stayed put. He put his hands on his hips and stared at his brother.

"You're not going to do anything stupid, are you?" he asked Jake.

"I'll take care of the situation," Jake answered, causing Royce to curse.

Royce's gaze snapped to her. "Whatever the hell he's thinking about doing, talk him out of it." And with that *farewell,* Royce hurried after Nell and Sunny.

Jake and she went to the kitchen, and from the window they watched as the SUV drove away on the back road that Jake and she had taken to get to the house.

Maggie glanced at Jake to see how he was handling this. He looked stoic enough, but she knew deep down his heart was breaking. He loved Sunny more than life itself, and his baby was in danger not just from her illness but from an old threat that seemingly wouldn't go away.

Well, not without help, it wouldn't.

"She'll be okay," Maggie whispered to Jake, and she hoped that was true. She paused, trying to find the right words, or rather the right argument, to convince him of what she had to do. "David called Royce, but you and I both know he really wants to talk to me."

"No—"

"And I want to talk to him," she finished, speaking right over Jake. "I can assure him the evidence against him is safe, and it'll stay that way."

"No," Jake repeated. He took her by the shoulders and roughly turned her around to face him. "You're going to stay here, and I'll go out there to talk to David."

Now it was her turn to take him by his arms. "The marshals are after you," she reminded him.

"I'll only be out there a few minutes. I just want to hear what he has to say."

"What he has to say?" she repeated, practically in a shout. "He probably wants to kill you in retaliation for the pact I broke with his father."

"I'm not going out there unarmed, and he won't get a chance to kill me. If he draws his gun, I will, too, and we'll end this here and now."

Maggie noted the stubborn set of his jaw and gave it right back to him. "It won't end it. If you hurt David or kill him, that'll just unleash Tanner. He'll come after you with all he's got."

"He's already come after us with that gunman I left dead in the woods. Now, I just need to figure out who Tanner's using to try again. If it's Dr. Grange, then I have to know so I can have him arrested for aiding a convicted felon."

Maggie could see that side of the argument, but there was a more obvious side. "You really think David will tell you who his father hired to hurt us?"

"Not intentionally, but I'll try to light a fuse or two to his temper and see what comes out of his mouth."

Maggie just shook her head. "Anything that comes out of David Tanner's mouth will be a lie designed to protect his own butt or his father's."

"Maybe. But it'll only cost me a few minutes of my time. Then, we're getting out of here. I have to get you to someplace safe."

He didn't say where that place might be, perhaps because a safe one didn't exist. Still, almost anywhere was safer than here since it was the first place Tanner's men would look. The marshals, too. Maggie seriously doubted that they'd stay away for long, because they would be antsy to talk to Jake and arrest him.

"The ranch hands are out there to back me up," he added. Jake took a pair of walkie-talkies from the foyer desk drawer and handed her one. "I'll keep it on so you can hear what he says. Be ready to leave as soon as I get back."

And that was it. He certainly wasn't asking her permission to attend this meeting. Jake gave her one last look and headed out the door.

Maggie hurried to the window, keeping out of sight but peeking around the edge of the window frame so she could keep watch. She wished she had a gun so she could give Jake some backup, but Jake had taken back his Beretta.

At least the two ranch hands out there were well armed, and while David might have criminal intentions, he wasn't stupid. Far from it. He wouldn't fire on Jake if there was a chance he could be gunned down himself.

As Jake approached him, David lifted his hands in the air, no doubt to show Jake that he wasn't armed. However, the man was wearing a thick duster-length coat. He could conceal a grenade launcher in that garment.

"Jake," she heard David say when Jake stopped in front of him. "Thank you for agreeing to speak with me."

"You said you had information to save my daughter." There was nothing friendly about his tone, and he certainly didn't acknowledge the thank-you.

"I do." David made an uneasy, sweeping glance around them and lowered his hands to his side. "Just so you know, my father didn't send me, and if he knew I was here, he wouldn't be pleased."

"Really?" Jake challenged.

"Really," he confirmed. "I came to warn you that my father had a large sum of money transferred from one off-shore account to another. In the past, he's only done that for one reason—to pay someone to do something illegal for him."

Oh, mercy. Maggie didn't doubt that Tanner had done

such a thing, but she was seriously doubting David's motives for telling Jake.

"I need the name of the person he hired." Jake asked.

David shook his head. "I've been trying to find out but so far, nothing."

Jake said something she didn't catch. "So, you came here out the goodness of your heart to warn me of the obvious—that your father's a cold-blooded killer?" He took a step closer, probably violating David's personal space. "I know what Tanner is. And I also know you're his son and would do anything for him."

"No. Not anymore." David made a weary sound and scrubbed his hand over his face. "Look, I don't expect you to believe that I want to do something to help you. I've given you no reason to trust me."

"You're right about that," Jake answered.

David looked him straight in the eyes. "But I *am* going to help you."

"The only help I want from you is information. Why were you skulking around town this morning?"

Maggie wished she were closer so she could see David's exact expression, but she thought maybe he flinched. "You mean my visit to Dr. Grange?" He lifted his shoulder. "I'd heard you were looking for a bone marrow donor for your daughter, and I had the test done, to see if I'm a match."

Well, Maggie hadn't seen that coming, but since it was coming from David, it could be a hollow gesture or even an attempt to cover up the real reason for the visit—an intimidation tactic to get information from the doctor. Still, if by some miracle he was a match and she wasn't, then one way or another she would get that bone marrow for Sunny.

"I'll let you know how the test turns out," David continued, "but I'm guessing your best bet is Maggie, since she and your daughter are blood kin. And that brings me to another reason why I'm here. There are rumors she's back."

"She's not," Jake lied. "She's in WITSEC, and she has a no-contact order against me and my family."

David nodded, indicating he knew that. "But if she were to learn Sunny was sick, she'd come back." He paused. "That wouldn't be a good idea."

"Because you'd try to kill her."

"No," David quickly disagreed. "But my father would use money from that offshore account to hire someone to do the job." Another pause. "And he would do that even if it meant Maggie had some kind of incriminating information against me."

Jake huffed loud enough for her to hear. "You want me to believe that your father would allow you to go to jail so he could get back at Maggie?"

"Yes." David didn't hesitate, either. "My father and I had a parting of the ways about three months ago."

"What caused that?"

David shook his head. "I'll plead the Fifth there. But let's just say it would have involved someone's death, and I wanted no part in it."

Maggie wasn't buying any of this.

"Maggie's death?" Jake pressed.

"No. Someone involved in my father's appeals process. Don't worry. The death didn't happen, and now I'm his scapegoat. Whatever evidence Maggie has against me," David continued, "my father will gladly stand back and let her use it if he doesn't have her gunned down first. He hates her, Jake. Not just for the investigation, but he blames her for his being on death row."

"Murdering my wife put Tanner on death row," Jake pointed out.

Maggie's chest tightened, and she felt sick to her stomach. She hated that Jake had to be reminded of Anna's death, but then Anna was no doubt always on his mind.

"And my father deserves to be where he is," David conceded.

David was giving a very convincing performance. She made a mental note to try to find out if there had indeed been some kind of falling-out between father and son. Maybe the prison officials would know.

"There's a lot I'm just learning about Maggie's investigation," David said a moment later. "How much has she told you?"

Had her heart stopped for a few seconds? It certainly felt like it.

Oh, sweet heaven.

Maggie wanted to shout out for David to keep his mouth shut. Jake didn't need this now. But if David knew, then eventually it would get back to Jake.

She needed to be the one to tell him.

It would only make things worse, of course. That seemed to be all she could do when it came to Jake—make things worse—and he might hate her all the more for keeping something like this from him.

"All of this is just talk," Jake said, "and I have a lot more important things I need to be doing." He turned to walk away.

"I can find out who my father hired to come after Maggie," David said.

That stopped Jake in his tracks, and he turned back around to face the man. "How? If you're on the outs with your father, as you say you are, why would he give you that kind of information?"

"He wouldn't give it to me," David verified. "But I still have access to some of his old contacts." He checked his watch. "Give me a couple of hours, and I'll have a name for you. Maybe then you'll see I'm trying to help you."

With that, David turned and walked to his car.

Chapter Seven

Jake glanced around the hunting cabin and hoped he hadn't made a huge mistake bringing Maggie here. Of course, anything he did at this point could turn into a huge mistake, so he just took a deep breath, unlocked the door and ushered her inside.

Maggie glanced around the place. Not that her glances could go far. There was a set of bunk beds and a couple of chairs on one side and a small kitchen and table on the other. The equally small bathroom was at the back, and there wasn't even a door to close it off, just a sliding curtain.

"We should only have to be here one night," he reminded her.

If that.

It was still a little before five, and if the test results turned out to be a match, they could be on their way to the hospital in the nearby town of Corner's Lake where Jake had arranged for the marrow harvesting. There were several hotels in the town, but he hadn't wanted to risk taking Maggie there just yet. Jake figured Tanner's goons would be watching the hospitals.

Watching for Maggie and him, too.

But thankfully Royce, Nell and his father had managed to sneak Sunny into an Amarillo hospital under a fake name. Staying there meant it would essentially tie up his family since they couldn't risk leaving, and that meant Jake had no real backup. There was only one other night deputy, Billy Kilpatrick, and he'd have to man the sheriff's office on his own.

Jake set the bags on the kitchen table, locked the door and set the security alarm he'd had installed the year before when they'd had a problem with kids vandalizing the place. The cabin wasn't on a path, beaten or otherwise, but he knew there was a chance that someone could still find them there.

Especially someone who was looking hard.

Maggie knelt down and turned on the electric heater. It would keep them from freezing, but he doubted it would make the place warm. No. They were in for a long, cold night. And the weather was only partially responsible for that.

Sunny's condition had certainly made Maggie and him strange bedfellows. Or rather bunk mates. At least they wouldn't actually have to share a bed.

Jake was beyond thankful for that.

He blamed that on the small quarters and the clothes that Nell had lent Maggie. When she'd been wearing the ugly waitress uniform, he hadn't been able to see much of her body. But he did now because she was wearing slim jeans. She also had a sweater and coat, but they, too, seemed to skim her curves. It was a stupid reminder that she was an attractive woman, and Jake told himself it was a reminder he was going to forget. *Now.*

"I need to clean something," Maggie said, rubbing her hands down the side of her coat. "It helps me relax."

Well, that was a first, and even though Jake didn't see the need to clean the temporary quarters, he tipped his head to the sink. "There should be some supplies in the cabinet beneath."

She gave him a shaky nod and didn't waste any time taking out some paper towels and a bottle of spray cleaner. Maggie stepped into the bathroom to tackle the sink that probably didn't even need cleaning. While she did that, he took out the food and extra blankets they'd packed. The extra weapon and ammunition, too.

He heard Maggie mumbling something and looked at her through the narrow opening of the bathroom. Her back was to him, her attention focused on the sink. She stopped, turned slightly, leaning her shoulder against the wall, and she touched the back of her hand to her mouth.

Maybe to choke back a sob.

He didn't go to her, but he didn't turn away, either. Jake watched her from the corner of his eye, but he also kept taking out the supplies so she wouldn't get suspicious from the sudden silence. Maggie didn't need to know he was gawking at her.

She kept her hand pressed to her mouth for several moments, but her gaze drifted to the denim shirt that was a peg on the wall.

His shirt.

He'd left it there months ago, the last time he'd used the cabin. She might have recognized it since he'd worn it a lot over the years.

With the paper towel in her right hand, she set the cleaning bottle in the sink, reached out with her left and skimmed her finger over the shirtsleeve.

Oh, man.

He hadn't expected a reaction to that, but he got one. It felt as if she'd touched *him*.

Her fingers slid from the sleeve to the collar. But not

just the collar. Inside it, along the neck. He got another punch of heat that he didn't want.

And then he saw something else.

The look on her face. Not fear, or the aftermath of a near sob. But the look of a woman remembering something. A touch. A kiss, maybe. Whatever was on her mind, his shirt had brought it all back.

Her mouth opened slightly, and he heard her breath. Saw the slight tremble of her mouth. She drew back her hand, touching her lips with her fingertips. Not like before…

It was more a memory she was reliving.

Jake was suddenly reliving it, too. He could feel her in his arms. The way she'd fitted against him—the softness of her breasts against his chest. The taste of her. Man, that taste had haunted him.

Still did.

Her fingers slipped from her mouth. To her bare throat. Before she slid her hand over her breast and to her belly, where she flattened her palm.

Yeah, Jake felt her there, too.

In his belly. And lower. She didn't move her hand lower, but Jake's mind seemed to be filling in the blanks. Imagining it, his mouth went dry. The blood started to pump fast through him. And, damn, he got an erection. That stupid part of him didn't know when to lie low.

When Sunny was better, he really needed to be with a woman. Not Maggie. But someone.

The buzzing sound shot through the room, and for a moment Jake thought it was all in his head. It wasn't. It was his new phone. One of those prepaid cells that couldn't be easily traced. He'd set it up so that any call made to the house phone or his other cell would be forwarded to him. Good thing, too, because he recognized the number of the caller. It was Tommy Rester, and Jake was glad for the interruption.

"It's me," Jake answered. Maggie came back into the room, but Jake turned away from her so she wouldn't see the obvious bulge behind his zipper. "Please tell me you have good news."

"Not yet. I got the blood to the lab, but there's only one tech working, and she's doing something on a high-profile murder case."

Yeah, definitely not good. "Can you press her to run it?"

"I am pressing," Tommy insisted, "but tomorrow's Christmas Eve, and she's not happy about working any later than she already is."

Jake tried to hold back the fear that rose inside him. "Just try," Jake said, "and if necessary I'll resort to begging or bribes." Hell, he'd already broken the law once, and he'd break it a dozen more times to save Sunny.

"I take it that wasn't David with the name he promised?" Maggie asked. She didn't seem to notice his erection, thank goodness, but there was a slight tremble in her voice when she said David's name.

It was a reminder of his conversation with Tanner's son. Jake figured most, if not all, were just lies to cover for Tanner or maybe just to torment him. Except for that one thing.

There's a lot I'm just learning about Maggie's investigation. How much has she told you?

It was a puzzling comment and maybe designed to get Jake thinking about things that shouldn't be occupying his thoughts. A distraction that would prevent him from seeing the real truth—that both Tanner and his son were very dangerous men.

"It wasn't David," Jake explained to her. "And even if he does call, I'm not holding out much hope that he'll give us anything." Especially the name of the person his father had hired to kill Maggie and anyone else he felt like killing. "That was the ranch hand who took your blood sample to the crime lab. He's working on getting it processed."

"Working on it," Maggie repeated in a mumble, and she started scrubbing the sink in the kitchenette. If she kept it up, she'd have scrapes and bruises on her hands.

Jake reached out and took her arm to stop her.

She looked up at him, shook her head. "It's just so hard being here."

Yeah, but Jake wasn't sure they were hard for the same reasons. But then, she glanced down. At his zipper.

Maggie blinked and did a double take.

"An involuntary reaction," he grumbled.

Her forehead bunched up. "To me?"

More than anything he wanted to deny it, but he doubted Maggie would believe he'd gotten that *reaction* from anything else in this man-cave of a cabin.

"I see," she said, and Jake knew his silence was the loudest of confirmations. "Funny, I was just thinking about, well, about a lot of things." She put the cleaning supplies on the counter and fluttered her fingers toward the bathroom. "Your shirt's in there, and it's the one you were wearing when you kissed me. I had an *involuntary reaction* to it."

If he hadn't seen her touch it, this would have been a very confusing conversation. But if he hadn't seen that, or the way she'd touched herself, he wouldn't have this asinine erection.

"You don't know how many times I had to force myself not to lust after my sister's husband," she said. She waved him off before he could answer that, but the wave was for no reason because Jake didn't have an answer for it anyway. "Old water, old bridge."

But the attraction was still there.

"You're the one who left Mustang Ridge after you finished college," he reminded her.

She nodded. "To move to Amarillo. I wanted to be a cop and I wasn't sure you'd hire me."

"You didn't ask."

Another nod, followed by a sound in her throat. "Didn't think it was a good idea. Besides, by then Anna had told me she wanted you."

Jake didn't doubt that. Ten years ago if someone had asked him which Gallagher sister he would have ended up with, he would have said Maggie. But after she'd left town and focused on her career, Anna and he had started spending more time together. Had gotten closer. And eventually Anna had gotten pregnant.

That's when Jake had proposed.

And he didn't regret it or the pregnancy.

"It all worked out," she said. "Well, in some ways. You got Sunny."

Yeah. And even though his marriage to Anna hadn't been perfect, not by a long shot, Sunny was worth it.

Maggie stepped back, though the small space didn't allow her to go far. "Sunny's so sick." And that's all she said for several moments. "I mean, you warned me, but seeing her..."

"Yeah," Jake settled for saying.

"This is all my fault. If I hadn't done that investigation, Anna would be alive and probably a match. Sunny would already be well."

Jake automatically stiffened at the sound of his late wife's name. A conditioned reflex. Like the punch of pain and hatred he felt. But it was hard to hang on to that hatred when Maggie was risking her life. It didn't make up for what had happened, but it wasn't something Jake could just push aside.

Neither was the tear that spilled down her cheek.

Cursing, he reached for her, but Maggie batted his hands away. "I'm not tough like I use to be. If I lean on your shoulder, I might not be able to quit leaning."

Jake knew that was a huge confession coming from the woman who never showed any signs of weakness. Worse, he was afraid it might be true. That, however, didn't stop Jake from making what was probably a huge mistake.

He reached out, put his arm around her and pulled Maggie to him so she could use his shoulder.

It didn't help her tears. They came faster and harder now until she was sobbing. Jake didn't try to stop her because he'd had his own battle with coming to terms with how sick Sunny was. Maggie had only had hours to adjust and, during that time, someone had tried to kill her.

"Sorry." She pushed herself away from him and used one of the paper towels to dry her face. "Just what you need right now—a woman blubbering all over you and giving you…involuntary reactions."

No, he didn't need it, and Jake didn't need the reminder of how Maggie felt in his arms. He'd held her like this two months after Anna's death, when they'd both been so racked with grief. She'd had his shoulder then, too.

And his mouth.

Hell, she'd had a lot of him since Jake had been ready to forget everything and lose his mind in her body.

"Yes," Maggie mumbled as if she knew what he was thinking. And maybe she did. Because Jake could have sworn that the thought of those memories changed the air between them.

It suddenly didn't seem so freezing cold.

Maggie shoved her hands in her coat pockets and drew in a deep breath. "We should eat or something."

But she didn't move. Nor did she look at the food that

Jake had placed on the table. Jake didn't, either. But he did do something, and he was a hundred percent certain that it was wrong.

Before he could talk himself out of it, he hooked his arm around Maggie's waist and yanked her to him. His mouth went to hers. Not for some gentle kiss between lovers.

No.

There was no gentleness between them, and in that moment Jake wasn't sure if this was about the heat between them or the pain this heat had caused.

He kissed her hard. Punishing both of them with the way he slammed her body against his. He wasn't sure who he wanted to hurt more—her or himself. He settled for hurting both of them, and he poured all the pain, the grief and the anger into that kiss.

Maggie took everything he dished out to her, everything, and she didn't try to push away. Just the opposite. Her fingers dug into shoulder, pulling him closer, until he felt his muscles cramp there. In the back of his mind he figured he'd have bruises.

He deserved worse.

He deserved the physical scars to go with the raw emotions he felt.

Maggie made a soft, helpless sound. The kind a person might make if they were drowning and there was no hope of survival. It was that sound of surrender that had him breaking the kiss, and Jake stared down into her eyes.

He should tell her he was sorry for the kiss, but the words wouldn't help. They were past that now. So, he leaned in and pressed his lips to hers. He didn't touch her with his hands. Nor with his body.

Jake just kissed her.

It was slow. Lingering. And he let the taste of her slide

through him. Yeah. He remembered that taste. Remembered how it had made him burn. It still did.

Maggie made another sound. Not surrender. But one of pure pleasure, and she deepened the kiss. Jake was a willing participant, however, and he did some deepening of his own.

He came to his senses. Not slowly. It hit him like a heavyweight's fist, and this time he did step way back from her.

They stood there, their breathing hard. Every part of them was primed for something that wouldn't happen.

"Don't you dare apologize," she said, and it wasn't a weak mumble, either. It sounded a lot like the old Maggie, the one who didn't work in the Tip Top Diner.

The formidable Maggie.

"The same goes for you," he answered.

And much to his surprise, Jake realized he didn't sound like a grieving widower but more like the man who'd felt he could weather anything. He didn't consider that a good thing. Not now anyway, when it could break down barriers between Maggie and him.

He needed those barriers to keep Anna in his heart.

Jake's phone buzzed again. And this time he didn't recognize the number. He pressed the answer button and put the call on Speaker so that Maggie could hear.

"It's me, Wade," the caller immediately said.

Well, Jake had intended to call the young man for questioning, but apparently Wade had beat him to him.

"We need to talk." There was a frantic edge to Wade's voice.

"I'm listening."

"No," Wade argued. "I mean I need to see you. We need to talk in person."

"That can't happen, but I do need to know something—

how fast did you go to Tanner after you hacked into the Justice Department files for me?"

"I didn't go to him," Wade snapped. "In fact, Tanner's the reason I'm calling you. Someone's been following me, and I got a glimpse of the guy, and he was carrying a gun."

Jake didn't like the sound of that, if Wade was telling the truth. "Who was he?"

"I don't know. Never seen him before in my life, but I think Tanner might have hired him. I mean, we already know the guy's a killer."

"Yeah, but he's got no reason to come after you," Jake pointed out.

"You're wrong. David called me and said his father might be riled that I helped you find Maggie Gallagher."

"David called you?" Jake repeated.

"To warn me," Wade clarified.

Jake figured that David had made it sound like a warning, but David was a Tanner, and he could have had another motive for contacting Wade. What that motive might be, Jake didn't know, but he wasn't about to trust David or his father.

Or Wade.

"David said I should get out of town for a while or lie low," Wade went on. "It's nearly Christmas. Hardly the time for leaving town. And that's why I called you. I want some kind of police protection from Tanner. The man scares me."

Jake groaned. He didn't have the energy for this, especially since it could all be act. Still, he was the sheriff for a little while longer anyway, and if something bad did indeed happen to Wade, it would be on his hands. He was already wrestling with enough guilt without adding that.

"I'll call Royce and see what kind of arrangements we

can make," Jake said. "In the meantime, David was right about staying low."

"Thanks." But Wade didn't sound appreciative. "Did the information I hacked help you find Maggie?"

"Not yet," Jake lied. "I'm still looking."

Without adding more or even saying goodbye, he clicked the end-call button and immediately phoned his brother. After he'd verified that Sunny was still all right, that her condition hadn't changed, he asked Royce to call Sheriff Logan over in Corner's Lake.

"You really think Wade needs protection from Tanner?" Royce asked.

"No. But I don't want him dead, either. It's an outside shot, but Tanner might consider Wade to be some sort of loose end."

"Yeah," Royce agreed. "Or maybe Wade is just trying to muddy the waters."

Jake had considered that, too. "If Sheriff Logan can provide a protection detail, try and get updates on Wade's whereabouts. I'd like to keep any eye on him, too."

"Will do. Any word from Dr. Grange on those lab results?" Royce asked.

"Not yet." Jake checked the time. "But I'll go ahead and give him a call." He paused. "Tell Sunny I love her."

"Already have," Royce promised, "but I'll tell her again. How's Maggie holding up?"

"I'm fine," she jumped to answer.

Jake glanced at her mouth that was slightly pink from their rough kissing session. She wasn't fine. Neither was he. That kiss had rattled both of them in part because it'd lit some very bad fires in his body.

And he was pretty sure that kiss wasn't the last.

"Sunny asked about you, Maggie," Royce added.

Maggie pressed her hand to fore chest as if to steady her

heart, and she smiled. However, that smile faded when she glanced at Jake. Probably because he had a scowl or something on his face. That was his usual reaction when he had Sunny and Maggie in the same thought. But he wanted to kick himself now because, after all she was doing for Sunny, Maggie didn't deserve to be scowled at.

"What did Sunny say?" Maggie asked, her voice tentative and so was the second glance she gave him.

Royce cleared his throat. "She wanted you to read a story to her. And she mentioned something about you being at the ranch with her for Christmas. A present to her, she said."

Just like that, Maggie's expression changed, and he saw the sadness creep into her eyes. Probably because spending Christmas together wasn't possible. If they had the match and the bone marrow by then, Maggie would be on her way back into WITSEC. Jake refused to consider that she wouldn't be a match.

"Tell Sunny I'll call her on Christmas," Maggie finally said. "And tell her I love her."

"I will," Royce assured her, and he ended the call.

"A present?" Jake questioned.

Maggie nodded but couldn't hide the wince that crossed her face. "Sunny did ask if I could stay, but I didn't say yes." She dodged his gaze, turned away from him. "She also asked if I could be her mommy."

Jake groaned before he could stop himself.

"I know," Maggie jumped to say. "I'm so sorry." And she just kept repeating it while those tears threatened again. "I didn't bring it up, and I didn't do anything to encourage it."

"This isn't your fault," he heard himself say. It was the truth, but he figured that kiss had something to do with his blurting that out. "Lately, she's been asking a lot about her mother."

When Maggie continued to shake her head as if still blaming herself, Jake pulled her right back in his arms. Oh, yeah. It was stupid. His body was still tingling from their kiss, and holding her was only complicating the situation.

Except it was different this time.

Not sexual, exactly. Something more. Something Jake damn sure didn't want to feel because it was like a betrayal to Anna. He released the grip on her and stepped back so fast that he was certain she'd ask for some kind of explanation. And maybe she would have if his phone hadn't buzzed.

He was actually grateful for interruption, until he heard the familiar voice on the other end.

"Jake, it's me, David."

"I'm surprised you called," Jake commented.

"I said I would. I don't have the bone marrow test results back yet, but I talked with some of my father's business associates."

"And?" Jake prompted when he didn't continue.

"And I have a name for you. I know who my father hired to kill you."

"You mean the man he hired to kill Maggie," Jake corrected.

"No," David corrected right back. *"You."*

Chapter Eight

Dr. Gavin Grange.

His name kept going through Maggie's head. So did the warning that David had issued several hours earlier with his call: his father, Bruce Tanner, had hired the doctor to kill Jake. She wanted to dismiss it as a total lie, especially since she didn't trust David one bit. But this sounded exactly like a plan Tanner would have concocted.

Use a person that Jake trusted. A person he would have contact with because of Sunny's illness. It was smart and sick, two things that Tanner was good at.

"Top or bottom?" she heard Jake say.

Maggie had no idea what he meant, and she jerked her attention to him. Since they hadn't wanted to risk using the overhead light, the only illumination in the room came from the orangey coils on the heater, but Maggie saw that he was looking at the bunk beds. Her mind hadn't been on that steamy kiss or his *involuntary reaction,* but it was now, even though it was clear that Jake's question had no sexual meaning.

Since David's call, Jake had given her a wide berth. Jake was no doubt trying to decide what, if anything, he should do with the accusation about the town's doctor.

"I'll take the bottom," she answered.

Maggie stepped away from the tiny heater that was providing the only warmth for the cabin, and she grabbed one of the blankets Jake had brought with them.

"You okay?" Jake asked as he eyed her suspiciously.

She nodded, not wanting to rehash David's call, their kiss or the fact they hadn't heard back on any of the test results. They both had enough weighing on their minds without discussing the details.

Maggie climbed beneath the covers that were already on the bed. Cold covers, she quickly realized. It was like sleeping in snow, and the extra blanket that Jake helped spread over her didn't add much warmth. He lifted an eyebrow when she started to shiver.

"I'll be fine," she lied again.

He made a *suit yourself* sound and climbed onto the top bunk. Jake didn't say good-night, probably because they both knew it wouldn't be one, and it would take a miracle for either of them to get any sleep.

The minutes crawled by, but they weren't crawling fast enough. Since nightfall, the temperature had steadily dropped, and even though she still had on her clothes and coat, her teeth started to chatter. Great. No way to hide that sound in the otherwise quiet cabin.

She tried to get her mind on something else. Maggie went back to that kiss and wished she had that kind of heat again.

Yeah, it was stupid to wish that, especially since it wasn't just about keeping warm. Being with Jake had made her remember how hollow her life was. It was a good thing she wouldn't be going back to Coopersville, because she seriously doubted she could make it work.

One more butt pinch from Herman Settler, and she'd probably lose it.

Above her, she heard Jake mumble some profanity, and

he climbed down from the bunk. He piled all his covers on top of her. "Move over," he insisted.

He probably couldn't see her expression, but Maggie was sure he knew what was there. Skepticism, worry and, yes, some fear. "This is not a safe thing to do."

Jake slid her over himself and dropped down on the narrow mattress next to her. "Neither is catching pneumonia or getting frostbite. You're cold. I'm cold. We're stuck here until at least morning with no other blankets, and this is the only thing that makes sense.

"Besides, we've got on so many layers of clothes that we might as well be wearing chastity belts," he added in a mumble.

Maggie wasn't so sure of that, at all.

He turned onto his side, his back to her, and because there was no room between them, Maggie had no choice but to have her body against his.

Instant warmth.

And more than that, unfortunately.

Mercy, he smelled good. It was Jake's own scent mixed with Nell's Christmas gingerbread cookies they'd eaten earlier, and she had to force herself not to press closer to him to take in more of that. Apparently, she now had a thing for Jake's scent and had come way too close to sniffing his shirt that was hanging in the bathroom.

Yes, definitely a long night.

She should have been exhausted, but she couldn't even seem to close her eyes so Maggie just lay there next to Jake. Soon, she picked up the rhythm of his breathing, and she felt her own muscle start to relax a little.

"Why would Tanner choose to kill me?" Jake asked.

Clearly, she wasn't the only one struggling with sleep, and it was a question that she was mulling over, as well. Unless…

Maggie went back to the first kiss nearly two and a half years ago. Tanner had learned about that kiss because he'd taunted her with it when she'd visited once in the jail. Perhaps Tanner thought she was in love with Jake and that killing him was the best way to strike at her?

But she kept that to herself.

"Maybe even Tanner's not so twisted to go after a sick child," she suggested. "Or he might feel if he eliminates you, then it'll be easier to go after the rest of us. After all, you're the strong one. The alpha male. And in Tanner's eyes, his biggest threat."

Jake stayed quiet for so long that Maggie thought it might be the end of a conversation they probably shouldn't be having anyway. "I wasn't a threat to him when he went after Anna."

"You were. He didn't want you around to figure out what he was doing, but I think he was counting on bringing you to your knees just long enough for him to cover his tracks and get away with murder. But that didn't happen."

"Oh, I was brought to my knees all right. Tanner was a free man for two months. If I'd been thinking straight, I would have connected the dots sooner."

"Yes," she whispered. "And those dots led you to my investigation." Something that hadn't been readily apparent, not even to Maggie. "For the record, I didn't connect the dots, either. I didn't think Anna's death had anything to do with me or the investigation."

"Yeah." And there was another long pause. "I wasted two months believing her death had been some kind of random act of violence. That she'd been in the wrong place at the wrong time when that armed robber came into the store where she was. I was wrong."

"We both were," she added. "And we were both punished. Me, rightfully so. You, simply because of the fallout." The fallout was still there.

"What kept you from going off the deep end?" Jake asked.

It was an easy answer. "Punishment. I figured if I was dead, then that would be too easy. I didn't deserve easy."

"None of us deserved what we got."

"No." And that agreement hung between them for a while.

"I keep going back to David's comment," Jake said. "The part where he said he was just learning about your investigation and he wondered how much I knew. What did he mean?" he pressed. "And I'd rather hear it from you, rather than having to ask him."

Oh. Well, that took away her out. Or rather her lie that she had no idea what David was talking about. She definitely didn't want Jake bringing this up with David.

Heaven knew the spin David would put on the truth.

Maggie chose her words carefully. "Someone came to me with the initial information about Tanner's illegal activity, and I felt duty bound to investigate it because it was pretty clear that the guy was a crook."

And she froze, waiting for Jake's next question, and he didn't waste any time tossing it out there.

"Who came to you?"

Maggie tried not to waste any time, either. "I'd rather not say." In fact, she *wouldn't* say. "And I'd prefer if you didn't talk this over with David. Anything that comes out of his mouth would probably be a lie anyway."

Or worse. A lie coated with a little bit of truth.

"Why won't you tell me?" Jake asked.

Oh, mercy. He just wasn't going to let this drop. "I promised to keep the informant's identity confidential."

Definitely the truth, and it was a promise Maggie intended to keep.

Despite everything that'd happened.

"Confidential," he repeated, mumbling some profanity. "Even now, that's between us. The secrecy. The pain. I know it's been two and a half years, but part of me wants to keep on hating you," Jake said.

Well, she'd gotten her wish about the end of a Tanner conversation, but this one could be just as lethal.

"Part of you should keep on hating me," she agreed.

Jake turned, slowly, easing himself around until he was facing her. "So, why did I kiss you then, huh? Why did I have that reaction to you?"

"Yet something else we shouldn't be discussing," she reminded him.

He stared at her, and in the dark room, she could barely make out his eyes. They were fixed on her, and even though she couldn't see the details of his face, she figured his forehead was bunched up. His mouth tight. Jaw muscles, too.

"I miss her every day," he whispered, his breath hitting against her mouth. Not quite a kiss but close enough for Maggie to get a whole lot warmer than she had been just seconds earlier.

Maggie made a sound of agreement. "Me, too." And maybe that would remind him, and her, of the pain that wasn't going away.

Jake cursed. It was bad. And he jerked away from her and turned his back to her again. This was better, Maggie said to herself.

Another lie.

But she'd told so many of them tonight, what was one more? She didn't want Jake to keep on hating her and she hadn't wanted him to turn away—again.

The quiet returned. The cold, too, and Maggie huddled against his back to keep herself warm. She forced herself to close to eyes. To clear her mind. She wouldn't do Sunny or Jake any good if she was sleep deprived.

"You know you'll have to tell me sooner or later," Jake whispered. "You'll have to tell me who asked you to investigate Tanner."

Maybe. But sooner wasn't going to be tonight. And if Jake thought the answer was going to give him some peace and ease some of his pain, it wouldn't.

In this case, the truth might destroy him.

Chapter Nine

The sound woke him.

Jake snapped to a sitting position, and in the same motion he drew his gun. Maggie moved, too, no doubt to get up and see what the heck was wrong, but he made a *shh* sound, and he turned his head, listening for whatever had made the sound.

Maggie and he waited, huddled on the bunk bed. However, the only thing Jake could hear was the wind battering the trees and the cabin.

It was morning, barely, and the sun was just starting to come up, which meant he didn't need to be sleeping anyway. He needed to call Royce to find out how Sunny was doing and if there'd been any progress with the test results.

He reached to pull back the cover but stopped when he heard the sound again. Definitely not the wind.

"I think it's a car engine," Maggie whispered.

Maybe, but if so it wouldn't be near the cabin, because there was no direct road to get there, just a ranch trail, and because of the ice it wasn't passable. Jake had parked his truck on the side of the ridge, and they'd walked the last eighth of a mile to the cabin.

He got up from the bunk bed, turned off the heater to silence the humming noise it was making, and he went to the window. With everything else going on, it was probably too much to hope that a hunter had just stumbled upon them by accident.

Maggie picked up the Colt that Jake had brought with them and went to the window over the sink to look out at that side of the cabin. Jake did the same at the front.

It was still dusky, with just a sliver of sunlight, making it hard for him to see anyone or anything. The same would be true for anyone out there. Plus, with the heater off, there were no lights on inside. Of course, if someone— Tanner's hired gun, for instance—had seen Jake's truck on the isolated trail, it wouldn't be hard to figure out that Maggie and he were in the cabin.

"See anything?" she whispered.

"No." But something wasn't right. "Stay here," Jake insisted.

She frantically shook her head. "You're not going out there."

"I just want to look around." And before Maggie could make another objection, Jake did just that.

He eased open the door. With the wind knifing through the room, the temperature started to plunge, and the cold gunmetal in his hand didn't help. If he didn't see anything in a second or two, he would shut the door. However, the thought had no sooner crossed his mind than he did see something.

Movement near one of the winter-bare cottonwood trees.

Maggie must have seen it, too, from the window. "There's someone out there."

Jake didn't have time to react to her warning. Because someone fired a shot.

He slammed the cabin door and scrambled toward Maggie. He hooked his arm around her and pulled her into the tiny recessed area between the living area and the bathroom.

It didn't get them away from the windows completely. There was still one on the far side of the bathroom, the one in the kitchen and the other at the front of the house. Still, with Maggie and him in the shadows, they would be harder to see. He hoped.

Of course, the shooter would be harder to see, too. But to get to Maggie and him, that shooter would have to come closer to the cabin. When that happened, Jake would have a shot of his own.

"Did you get a look at the guy?" Jake asked Maggie.

"No. I just saw the movement by the cottonwood tree." Her breath was gusting, and he figured she was primed and ready for a fight. He certainly was, and the adrenaline continued to pump right through him.

Who was out there?

And why had the person fired the shot?

As far as Jake could tell, the bullet hadn't gone into any part of the cabin, and while the place wasn't big, someone just yards away by the cottonwoods should have been able to hit it.

Jake braced himself for another shot, but one didn't come. The seconds ticked off in his head, turning to minutes, and he stepped forward just a little so he could get a look out the kitchen side window.

There.

He saw someone by the trees.

From the person's build, it appeared to be a man, but Jake couldn't tell if it was one of their suspects. Of course, it could be a hired assassin sent by Tanner.

Jake fastened his attention to the man. Waited more snail-crawling minutes. And he finally saw more movement. The guy dropped something on the ground and, much to Jake's surprise, he turned and started to run back down the ridge.

Hell.

What was going on?

"Wait here," he said to Maggie.

Jake hurried back to the door, opened it and looked around the area in front of the cabin. Nothing. Just the sound of running footsteps, and the person was headed right to the area where Jake had left his truck.

"I'm going with you," Maggie said when he went onto the porch.

Jake figured he could waste time arguing with her or just let her follow him. So he went with the second option. In the back of his mind, he reasoned that Maggie would be a good backup, but he didn't want her outside in direct danger. That's why he'd have to make this quick, with a look over the ridge, and then get her back inside. Of course, then they would need to grab their things and leave right away since their location had been compromised.

Maggie stayed right behind him as they trekked their way through the ice and snow. It wasn't deep, but it was enough for him to see the tracks the person had left behind. They did indeed lead to the ridge.

Jake slowed as they got to the rim, and he peered down at the trail below. Yeah. There was another vehicle and he didn't recognize it. He couldn't tell if the driver was already inside.

He heard the swishing sound to his right and, with his gun ready and aimed, he pivoted in that direction. The man was there. In a cluster of trees. And he must have spotted Jake and Maggie, too, because he turned to run.

Cursing, Jake ran after him.

Cursing, too, Maggie ran after Jake.

The guy wasn't very fast, and it didn't take Jake long

to catch up with him. He launched himself at the man and tackled him, and the impact sent them both crashing to the frozen ground. Jake saw a star or two when his shoulder collided with a rock, but he managed to hang on to the guy, and he dragged both himself and the man to their feet.

"Don't shoot!" the man shouted.

It was hard to see his face in the dim light and with the snow and ice on it, but Jake had no trouble recognizing that voice.

It was Wade Garfield, the man Jake had hired to break into the Justice Department files.

"Don't shoot," Wade repeated, and he lifted his hands in the air.

"You shot at us," Maggie snarled. She held the Colt on Wade while Jake gave him a quick pat down. It didn't take him long to find the small gun inside Wade's pocket.

"I didn't shoot at you," Wade argued. "It went off by accident. I'm not used to handling weapons."

Jake wasn't sure he believed that, but he had so many other questions that he pushed that one aside and started with the obvious.

"Why are you here, Wade?"

The young man huffed. "Because I was looking for you. I told you Tanner was trying to kill me, but you ignored me. Well, I won't let you do that now. You'll tell me what the heck is happening."

Since that was going to be one of Jake's questions to Wade, he mimicked the huff. "If you wanted police protection, why didn't you just go to the sheriff's office? The night deputy's there."

"So are those marshals. Two of them, and they're not saying what they want, but I figure it's me and you. They're here to arrest us, aren't they?"

"They're not after you," Jake assured him. "In fact,

there's nothing that can connect you to the hacking unless you tell them. That's why I used my own computer, not yours, and that's also why I won't say a word about you to the marshals or anyone else."

That didn't seem to calm Wade down any. He was shaking, but that could be from the cold, because Maggie was shaking, too. Jake didn't want to take Wade into the cabin, but by God he wanted some answers, and he didn't want Maggie to freeze to death while that happened.

"Follow me," Jake ordered the man, and he put Wade's gun in his pocket. If and when things settled down, Billy Kilpatrick, the night deputy, could check and see if Wade had a permit for the darn thing. Highly doubtful since Wade had claimed he didn't know how to use it.

Jake didn't reholster his gun. Neither did Maggie, and they ushered Wade into the cabin. She turned the heater back on while Jake put their guest into the chair so he could continue his unofficial interrogation. When he was done, he was either going to have to let Wade go or else call Billy and figure out a way to take the man into custody. Jake didn't relish the idea of arresting the man who'd helped him with that hacking, but he couldn't have people go around shooting, either.

"I want the truth." Jake took the other chair, whirled it around so the back was to Wade, and he sat, facing the man. "Did Tanner send you?"

"No! I've already said I've got nothing to do with him. Hell's bells, Sheriff, the man is on death row. Yeah, I hacked those files for you, and maybe I've done some things I wouldn't brag about to a lawman, but I'm not stupid. And I don't want any dealings with a man who'd gun down an innocent woman."

There was enough fire and maybe fear in his voice to

make it sound like the truth, but Jake wasn't ready to cross Wade off his suspect list just yet.

Since Maggie was glaring at Wade and still had her gun pointed at him, Jake figured she felt pretty much the same.

"How did you find us?" Jake asked.

Wade didn't jump to answer that question as he had the other. In fact, he leaned away from Jake and glanced at everything in the cabin but Maggie and him. It was enough of a reaction for Jake to curse.

"How?" Jake pressed.

"I'll tell you," Wade snapped. He tipped his head to Maggie. "But I want her to put away that gun first. I don't want to be shot for taking a precaution or two."

"A precaution?" Jake repeated. He didn't like the sound of that.

"The gun stays where it is," Maggie insisted. "Now start explaining." Even though she was still shivering, she managed to sound like a cop.

Wade drew in several very short breaths before his attention settled on Jake. "Night before last when you were at my place and we were hacking into the files, I put a GPS tracking device on your truck."

It took Jake a moment to process that, and he didn't process it well. "When the hell did you do that? And why? I especially want to know the *why*."

"I told you I had to use the bathroom, remember? Well, I sneaked outside and put the tracking device on the undercarriage of your truck."

Maggie moved closer, leaned in. "You keep spare tracking devices at your house?"

"I do," Wade said defensively. "Hey, I never said I was a Boy Scout. Sometimes, people come to me when they want to spy on their spouses. Or their exes. Hell, even their kids. For a fee, I help them out. I sell them the GPS and sometimes even hide it on the vehicles for them."

Jake jumped right on that. "Who paid you a *fee* to put that device on my truck?"

"No one." Wade got to his feet, but Jake put him right back in the chair. "I did it for my own protection."

Jake wasn't sure who huffed louder, Maggie or him. "Explain that," Jake insisted.

Wade gave a crisp nod. "I'd never done business with you before, and I didn't know if you were running some kind of sting operation. So, I recorded our conversation, in case I had to prove entrapment, and I put the tracker on your truck in case you ran off and left me holding the bag."

It'd been a first for Jake, too, to do business with a hacker, and if he hadn't been so desperate to find Maggie, he might have realized he couldn't trust Wade. He might have looked for things like recording and tracking devices. But he hadn't. And now, he had to consider what Wade had done—and would do—with that information.

Jake waited for Wade to say he wanted extra money, that he was blackmailing Jake, but he simply shook his head. "Will you give me police protection?" he asked.

Jake ignored him. "Where's the recording of our meeting?"

"In a safe place."

Maggie poked Wade's arm with her gun. "Where?" she demanded.

Wade winced and rubbed his arm even though Maggie had barely touched him. "At my house, okay? Jeez, I thought you'd still be all torn up about your sister's death. I didn't think you'd turn renegade cop."

"If I turn renegade, you'll be the first to know." Jake wasn't getting any positive vibes from Wade, and he figured that recording would come back to haunt him. He only hoped it didn't interfere in some way with Sunny getting the medical treatment she needed.

"Come on." Jake stood and yanked Wade to his feet. "Show me where you put the tracking device on my truck and then give me the laptop or whatever device you used to monitor the tracker."

"A laptop," Wade answered, his voice suddenly shaky again. "And it's in my car. If you take it, though, I'll expect some kind of payment. That laptop wasn't cheap."

Jake didn't want the laptop or the tracking device, but he wanted the latter off his vehicle. Once he had Wade on his way, Maggie and he would need to leave fast since Wade couldn't be trusted to keep something like that secret.

Jake took a small flashlight from their supply bag. "Why don't you wait here?" Jake suggested to Maggie.

She didn't. She turned off the heater again and followed him, of course, and the three of them went back into the cold.

"When you leave here," Jake said to Wade, "go to the sheriff's office and stay there. As soon as I can, I'll arrange protection."

Of course, just Wade showing up at the office and requesting protection would create a ton of questions, but Jake figured a resourceful guy like Wade could deal with that himself.

Jake stopped when he got to the cottonwood tree where he'd first seen Wade skulking around. With the shot being fired, the chase and interrogation, Jake had forgotten something that might turn out to be important.

He'd seen Wade drop or throw something on the ground.

Knowing Wade, it could be bad news.

"Wait," Jake insisted, and he snagged Wade by the coat while he had a look around. He finally spotted the small black object. It hadn't sunk down into the snow but was instead just sitting on top of it.

"Care to tell me what that is?" Jake asked.

Wade didn't even look at it. Definitely a bad sign.

Maggie inched closer for a better look. She studied it a moment and then whirled back around to face Wade. "That better not be what I think it is."

Jake took a harder look. "That's a GPS tracking device." And he was about to ask if it was the one from his truck and why it was there.

But Jake soon had his answer.

With the sun peeking up higher now, he saw the vehicle making its way up the trail to where Wade and he were both parked. Not just any ordinary vehicle, either. Black, nondescript.

The kind federal law enforcement officers used.

"I'm sorry," Wade said. "I had no choice. I took it off your truck and brought it up here so you'd be easier to find."

The car stopped, both doors swung open and the two men stepped out. Armed. And they immediately pointed their weapons at Jake.

"Drop your gun, Sheriff McCall," one of them shouted. "You're under arrest."

Chapter Ten

Maggie knew she had to do something to stop what had already been put into motion. Jake didn't deserve to be arrested. But first things first, she had to make sure this situation didn't escalate into a shooting.

She lifted her hands, so the marshals could see the weapon she held. Beside her, Jake did the same, and with their guns pointed right at Jake and her, the marshals made their way up the trail.

"Can I go now?" Wade asked one of the lawmen.

The taller one nodded, and Wade hurried away as if someone had lit fire to him. Maggie didn't want that to happen, not exactly, but she wouldn't mind blasting Wade for planting that GPS on Jake's truck and then leading the marshals right to them. Of course, better the marshals than Tanner, but still, this situation could get ugly.

"Maggie," the taller marshal greeted.

She released the breath she'd been holding because she recognized that voice. It belonged to Dallas Walker, the very officer who'd been monitoring her in WITSEC.

Maggie slipped the gun into her coat pocket. "You're a long way from Maverick County. Why did they send you?"

"I volunteered when I heard what happened." He was an imposing man, at least six-three, and even in the dim morning light, she could see the imposing glare he aimed at Jake. "I'm Deputy U.S. Marshal Walker, and this is my partner, Marshal Harlan McKinney, and you need to put down that gun. Use just two fingers and ease it onto the ground."

Oh, mercy. They were treating Jake like a common criminal.

The moment Jake put the gun on the ground, Marshal Walker took the cuffs from his belt and went toward him.

Maggie stepped in front of the marshal. "Jake did what he did to save my life."

"Maggie," Jake warned. "You don't need to do this."

"Hush," she warned him right back. She stared at the marshal. "Jake found out I was in danger, that Bruce Tanner had found my location and was going to send a gunman after me. When Jake couldn't find me, he went into my files so he could tell me."

"He did that to save you?" Harlan, the other marshal questioned.

Maggie nodded. Her breath was gusting now from the cold and the adrenaline, and she hoped she looked more confident about that answer than she felt.

The marshals exchanged glances. Walker mumbled something and he hitched his shoulder toward the vehicles. "Let's go to the sheriff's office and get this straightened out." He reached down and retrieved Jake's gun.

Jake just glared at her. "What do you think you're doing?" he said in an angry whisper as they made their way down the ridge.

"The right thing," she assured him.

Jake opened his mouth to argue with her, and she hooked her arm around him to pull him closer. "Think of Sunny. She needs you, and she won't have you if you go to jail."

There. That seemed to do it. Well, except that his muscles went rock hard. Jake had broken the law to find her, but lying about that seemed to be a higher crime for him. Maggie, however, thought the lies would be well worth it if they stopped this injustice from happening.

The marshals ushered them into the backseat of their vehicle and started the drive back down the ridge and toward town.

Marshal Walker met Jake's gaze in the mirror. "Your daughter's sick," he tossed out there like a gauntlet. "There's talk around town that you've been looking for a bone marrow donor for her."

"I have been." And that's all Jake said. His jaw muscles had tightened, his forehead had bunched up, and she was afraid at any second, he'd blurt out the truth.

"If you're implying that's why Jake found me," Maggie said, "you're wrong. It's true he did want me tested, but like I said, he found me to save my life."

"Talk is the sheriff hates you," Walker added.

Maggie was beginning to despise those who were doing all this talking. "He does," she readily admitted. Even though as she said that, she remembered the scalding kiss. And all that snuggling on the bunk bed. Still, there was some hate left. "But he saved my life by finding me."

With his partner behind the wheel, Walker turned in the seat and stared at her. "Can we cut the BS? The sheriff hacked into a classified database to locate you so he could have you tested as a bone marrow donor for his sick child."

"What would you have done in his place?" she snapped.

The staring continued before the marshal said something she didn't catch, and he turned back around. "Probably the same, but I can't give him a *get out of jail free* card on this. You could have been killed. I'm hearing reports of a gunman who attacked you right outside Coopersville."

"Did you find the body?" Jake asked. "Or better yet, did you confirm who hired him?"

"No to both questions, but I figure you know who we're dealing with—Bruce Tanner. He wants Maggie dead, and it was desperate and reckless for you to lead him to her." He cursed, shook his head. "Desperate anyway."

Yes, that pretty much described their situation.

The marshal drove down the trail and onto the farm road that rimmed McCall land. Maggie considered continuing the argument to get Jake free, but the timing was wrong. Mainly because Jake wouldn't let her have that argument. He wasn't just desperate, he was darn stubborn. Well, she was stubborn, too, and she wasn't dropping this without a fight.

By the time they arrived in town, the sun was already fully up, and while there was a dusting of snow, it wasn't as brutally cold as it had been the night before. A beautiful Christmas Eve morning. Or rather it would have been if not for Jake's and her situation.

The marshals both looked around Main Street, keeping watch. Maggie and Jake did the same, because Tanner was bold enough to hire someone to make an attack in broad daylight. However, there wasn't anyone out and about when Marshal McKinney brought the car to a stop directly in front of the sheriff's office.

Thank God, they didn't cuff Jake when they escorted him into the building, but Marshal McKinney kept a firm grip on Jake's arm.

The deputy, Billy Kilpatrick, had been asleep at the front desk, but he jumped to his feet when the bell over the door jangled. Maggie couldn't see or hear anyone else in the office, and it made her wonder where Wade had gone.

Obviously, not here.

So, maybe his request for protection had just been a

ruse to cover up his real reason for going to the ridge—to lead the marshals directly to Jake.

"You all right, Jake?" Billy asked.

Jake didn't answer, and McKinney led him to the interrogation room down the hall. Walker would have followed him if Maggie hadn't stepped in front of him and blocked his path.

Maggie looked at the deputy. "Billy, could you give us a minute?"

The man glanced around as if trying to figure out where to go. The Mustang Ridge sheriff's office wasn't a large building by any means. There was the entrance area with three desks for the dispatcher and two deputies. Down the hall was Jake's office, an interrogation room, a holding cell and a small break room.

"Maybe you can fix a fresh pot of coffee," Maggie suggested.

Billy nodded hesitantly and volleyed glances between her and the marshal before he left for the break room.

Maggie didn't waste any time. She looked Marshal Walker straight in the eye. "What will it take for you to let Jake go?"

"I can't," he said, not wasting any time, either.

"You can." She shoved her hair from her face. "He really did save my life."

He gave her a flat look. "And he really did hack into the database just to save you and not because he was looking for a bone marrow donor?"

"Why does it matter why he did it? He saved me."

"Yeah, after he put you in danger in the first place." His hands went on his hips. "Look, if it were up to me, I'd let him go. I do know the difference between justice and the law, and justice is a helluva lot more important. But there's no way I can justify to my boss that I didn't arrest the man who endangered someone in WITSEC."

"Yes, there is," Maggie said. She moved closer and lowered her voice to a whisper. "If Jakes goes free, I'll give you evidence that you can use to have David Tanner arrested. And when the times comes, I'll testify against him."

"Evidence?" he repeated.

"The kind that can put David in jail for a long time." She had to pause, gather her breath and pray that the marshal would snap this up. "Nearly two and a half years ago I cut a deal with Tanner to keep the evidence against his son a secret. In exchange, I agreed never to see the McCalls again. Well, the pact's been broken, and since Tanner seems bound and determined to kill Jake and me, then there's no reason for me to protect his son."

Walker stared at her and then groaned. "You should have told me this sooner, like two and a half years ago."

"I couldn't. I had to do something to keep the McCalls safe. And it worked. Until yesterday."

"Until Sheriff McCall allowed Tanner to find you."

"It wasn't like that," she argued. "I wanted to know about my niece. I want to try to save her, and there's no way Jake could have gotten the marshals to release my location since I had a no-contact order in my file."

He opened his mouth, no doubt to remind her the reason she had that no-contact order. It was because of Chet's threat to kill her. But it had also been so Maggie could cut herself off from the people she'd hurt.

"Please," she said.

The staring continued, and the seconds ticked off the clock. "Give me the evidence against David Tanner, and I'll keep it close to the vest until I can figure out how to use it without getting you killed."

"What about Jake?" Maggie pressed.

He had to get his teeth unclenched before he spoke. "Since I doubt you'll go back into witness relocation until this mess is resolved, I'm placing you in the sheriff's protective custody. No arrest, and in my report to my boss, I'll say that I believe some unknown perp used McCall's computer to hack into the database."

Her relief was so overwhelming that she caught on to the marshal's arm to steady her wobbly legs. "Thank you," she said.

"Don't thank me, because I'm not doing you any favors. Tanner will still come after you, and you and Sheriff McCall will have to figure out a way to stay alive and neutralize Tanner once and for all."

That would indeed be a Christmas miracle, but for now, Maggie was content with the gift the marshal had just given her.

"Oh, and don't contact anyone in the Marshals Service. I need to do some smooth talking to convince my boss that I did the right thing here, and he's off from work this week. Best if he doesn't have any input or contact with the sheriff or you."

Maggie nodded, and it wasn't a difficult agreement to make. She wanted the marshals out of the picture completely until she was positive that Jake wouldn't be arrested.

"We can help a little," the marshal continued. "We can take a harder look at Tanner's visitors at the jail, and if it appears he's sending out any messages for potential assassins, we can stop it."

Maggie doubted that would be nearly enough, but she kept those doubts to herself.

Walker turned and went to the interrogation room. While he was there, Maggie took a piece of paper from Billy's desk and jotted down the name of the bank and the number and password for one of the safety-deposit boxes where there were copies of David's signature on illegal land deals. There were two other sets of the info, but each deposit box had identical information.

Several moments later, Walker and McKinney came out of the interrogation room, and Maggie handed Walker the paper. "Thanks again," she whispered.

He certainly didn't issue a *you're welcome,* and Walker handed her both guns he'd taken from Jake and her, and the men walked out. Maggie didn't waste any time. She hurried back to the interrogation room, where Jake was mumbling profanities and pacing.

She braced herself for round two.

Jake glanced at the guns, and no doubt knew what that meant. "Damn it, Maggie, I didn't want you to lie for me."

"Oh, it's all right if you sacrifice yourself, but you won't allow it from anyone else. Well, relax. I didn't sacrifice anything. I'm doing something that I should have done a long time ago. I'm giving Marshal Walker the evidence I have against David."

Later, she'd deal with the fallout from that decision— from Tanner, David and even Jake. That evidence had a high price tag on it, and even though it would keep Jake out of jail, it would still hurt him. Badly.

Maggie pushed the thought aside. One battle at a time.

"We can't contact anyone in the Marshals Service until Walker gets everything straight. And he's going to help," she added, handing Jake his gun. She put the other in her coat pocket. "Walker will monitor Tanner's visitors and make sure he's not sneaking out any instruction to kill."

Jake stopped pacing and that seemed to get his mind back on Tanner and the threat he was to them. "He's probably getting the word out through his lawyers, and they can't monitor those conversations."

Send For
2 FREE BOOKS
Today!

I accept your offer!

Please send me two
free Harlequin Intrigue®
novels and two mystery
gifts (gifts worth about $10).
I understand that these books
are completely free—even
the shipping and handling will
be paid—and I am under no
obligation to purchase anything, ever,
as explained on the back of this card.

❏ I prefer the regular-print edition
182/382 HDL FNNH

❏ I prefer the larger-print edition
199/399 HDL FNNH

Please Print

FIRST NAME

LAST NAME

ADDRESS

APT.#   CITY

STATE/PROV.   ZIP/POSTAL CODE

Visit us online at
www.ReaderService.com

Send For
2 FREE BOOKS
Today!

I accept your offer!

Please send me two
free Harlequin Intrigue®
novels and two mystery
gifts (gifts worth about $10).
I understand that these books
are completely free—even
the shipping and handling will
be paid—and I am under no
obligation to purchase anything, ever,
as explained on the back of this card.

❏ I prefer the regular-print edition
182/382 HDL FNNH

❏ I prefer the larger-print edition
199/399 HDL FNNH

Please Print

FIRST NAME

LAST NAME

ADDRESS

APT.#	CITY

STATE/PROV.	ZIP/POSTAL CODE

Visit us online at
www.ReaderService.com

© 2011 HARLEQUIN ENTERPRISES LIMITED. ® and ™ are trademarks owned and used by the trademark owner and/or its licensee. Printed in the U.S.A. ▲ Detach card and mail today. No stamp needed. ▲ H+S13

"No, but they can monitor the lawyers, and if he meets with anyone that could be a suspected assassin, then they can bring the lawyers in for questioning."

He reholstered his gun, and the pacing returned. "It's dangerous for you to give up that evidence. It could have saved your life."

"And it could get me killed if David and his father are truly on the outs." She leveled her breath. Her emotions. And went closer to him. "It'd be more dangerous with you locked away. Do you think putting you behind bars will stop Tanner from coming after me and your family? No, it'll just make it easier. I want as many buffers as possible between Tanner and Sunny, and you and I make darn good buffers."

Maggie knew he couldn't argue with that, but it didn't mean Jake was happy about any of this. He didn't want to be in her debt, in any way, and she understood that. But she also understood that Jake would always put Sunny first.

"Thank you," he said. She heard the weariness and emotion in his voice. Felt the same in her own body.

She walked closer and risked touching his arm with just her fingertips. He didn't back away. In fact, he turned, slipped his arm around her and eased her to him.

"Thank you," he repeated. He brushed a kiss on her right temple. "If Chet were to see us like this, he'd blow a fuse."

"Then it's best we don't give him the chance." She'd tried to keep both her voice and the moment as light as possible, but she failed. Even though she'd known there could never be anything like a relationship between Jake and her, it hurt to think about what could have been.

She blamed that kiss in the cabin.

Twice she'd kissed Jake, and both times it had only made things worse between them. That should have been a lesson for her, but she didn't back away when Jake brushed another kiss on her cheek.

Just like that, Maggie felt her body go all warm and golden. It was a hunger. Always there. And touching him, with him holding her this way, only made the hunger worse.

"I watched you," he said. "When you were touching my shirt in the bathroom at the cabin."

Maggie lifted her head, looked at him and tried to recall everything she'd done during that touching session.

Oh, mercy.

She'd done *that*. She had pressed her hand to her stomach to try to ease the desire that thinking of Jake had created.

Jake glanced down between them at the specific parts of her she'd touched. There was no anger in his eyes now. Just that smoky, cool look that could have qualified as foreplay. He could seduce with those eyes alone, but he had so many more weapons in his arsenal.

That face, for one.

She wasn't sure how any guy could manage to look that hot with two days of stubble, but on Jake it always worked. So did the mussed hair. The mouth. His hands that were still gently bracketing her waist.

"That's why you got that…involuntary response?" she asked.

The corner of his mouth slid up. "That's as good a name for it as anything. It's been a while," he added in a whisper.

Sheez. That was not the right thing to say to her already aroused body. She was weak right now from the spent adrenaline and the worry. And an admission like that made her want to do something to erase that *a while*.

"That wasn't a request for pity sex," he let her know.

She nodded. "I think if we had sex, pity wouldn't play into it."

He nodded, too. Stared at her. And stared. The timing was so wrong it couldn't get any more wrong. Jake must have realized that because he stepped back so suddenly that Maggie staggered a little.

"Sorry," he said. "Sometimes, I forget."

She almost said *Forget what?* She suspected the answer was Anna, but fearing that it was his hatred of her instead, Maggie really didn't want to know.

Jake scrubbed his hand over his face, checked his watch. "I need to see Sunny."

She didn't question that, either, though it would take a lot of security measures for them to make a trip to the Amarillo hospital. Still, it'd be worth it. She needed to see Sunny, too.

Maggie heard the bell jangle, and someone opened the front door. Jake reacted instantly. After everything they'd been through, he obviously wasn't taking any chances. He shoved her behind him and drew his weapon.

"Sheriff McCall?" someone said.

It was Dr. Gavin Grange, and just the sound of his voice caused Maggie to take out her gun at well. The doctor's eyes widened, then narrowed, when he appeared in the doorway and spotted the drawn guns aimed right at him.

"You've both known me for over a decade," the doctor growled. "And I don't deserve this kind of treatment."

Neither Jake nor Maggie lowered their guns, and when Billy went by the door and saw what was going on, he drew, too.

"What's wrong?" Billy asked.

"I came to give them an update on the test results." Grange didn't say it nicely, either, and his eyes stayed narrowed.

"It's okay," Jake assured his deputy. "I can handle this."

"Now I require handling," the doctor spit out. "Well, believe what you will, but I'm not here to kill you."

"Maybe not," Jake answered. "And if that's true, then I'll apologize later. For now, Maggie and I need to take precautions, and you're included."

"Fair enough." But he didn't sound as if he believed it. "I came by to tell you that we should have the lab results this afternoon."

"Thanks. I appreciate that." And unlike the doc, Jake sounded genuine.

Grange stared at them for several more moments, turned as if to leave but then stopped. "Tanner's trying to set me up to make me look guilty of trying to kill you, but I don't want to harm anyone. I just want Tanner and his son out of my life."

Now, that was a strange thing to say.

"Other than David coming to see you about taking a bone marrow test for Sunny, I didn't realize they were *in* your life," Maggie commented.

"Or was David lying about that?" Jake pressed.

"He wasn't lying. Well, not that I'm aware of. He did take the test, but there aren't any results yet." Grange paused. "Yesterday morning, I visited Tanner at the prison."

Jake and she exchanged glances. "Why?" she asked.

"Because Tanner called and said it was critical that he see me. And no, he didn't ask me to kill you." The doctor shook his head. "I'm actually not sure what he wanted. He rambled on about a lot of things. His strained relationship with David, his exhausted appeals." Another pause. "And then he brought up Chet."

Maggie was sure she blinked. Because of Anna's murder, there was no love lost between Tanner and Chet, but

Maggie found it suspicious that Tanner would talk about him. Unless Tanner was going to make Chet a target.

Of course, the doctor could be lying about all of this.

"What did Tanner say about my father?" Jake asked when the doctor didn't continue.

"That's just it. He didn't say much of anything, other than that Chet had visited him."

Maggie glanced at Jake to see if he knew that'd happened, but he only shook his head. "When?"

"Don't know. Tanner wasn't clear about that. But he was clear on something else. He told me to give you two a message—that if you came to see him, he'd make it worth your while."

"How?" Jake immediately wanted to know.

"He said it was about following the money trail to find what you're looking for. And before you ask, I don't know what money, but I got the feeling he was talking about the threats to Maggie's life."

Probably. But she wondered why Tanner would give them info about that when he'd almost certainly been the one to hire the man who tried to kill them?

"Did Tanner happen to say what he and my father discussed?" Jake asked.

"Not directly, but he asked if I'd ever seen Chet at the clerk's office where Anna and Nell worked. I said I hadn't, but that it was highly likely he'd been there."

She wasn't sure any of this meant anything, but Maggie had the niggling feeling that it was important.

But how?

Why would Tanner have wanted to know something like that?

The answer flashed in her head. Anna and Nell often dealt with land records. One look at Jake, and she realized he was thinking the same thing.

"You think Tanner's worried that Chet saw something like the records for an illegal land deal?" Jake asked her.

"Maybe." But then she had to shake her head, too. "Why, though, would Tanner have waited all this time to say something about it?"

"Could be a veiled threat," Jake readily answered. "Or some kind of smoke screen meant to get us looking in the wrong direction."

That was true. Except Tanner had said Chet visited him. If Chet had indeed done that, then maybe Tanner had convinced him he had information that Chet needed.

Still, why keep the meeting a secret?

She figured Jake was asking himself the same thing.

"Ask your father about the meeting with Tanner," the doctor suggested. "And if I were you, I'd take every precaution, because Tanner came right out and said he wanted you dead." As David had done, Grange's attention was on Jake when he said that *you*.

"You want me to believe that Tanner doesn't want me dead?" Maggie asked.

"I'm sure he does, but he seemed more focused on hurting you than killing you. I think he blames you for the rift with his son."

"Me?" she questioned. "Before yesterday, I hadn't seen David since his father's arrest."

The doctor lifted his shoulder. "Just giving you my impression." His attention shifted back to Jake. "I'll call you when I have the results."

He walked away, and neither Jake nor she said a word until they heard the doctor leave.

"You believe everything he said?" she asked.

Jake blew out a long breath. "Tanner has a lot of money. Power, too. And he knows how to get to people." He checked his watch again. "But maybe talking to Tanner might help."

Maggie mentally replayed that to make sure she hadn't misheard him. "You want to see Tanner?"

"Yeah. And I want to see his face when I ask him about his visits with my father and Dr. Grange."

"You could just ask your father," Maggie pointed out.

"I could. But I'm not sure I'd get the truth about what they said to each other. I'm pretty sure we didn't get the truth from Grange." He stepped across the hall to his office and took a set of keys off the wall hook. "It's for an unmarked car," he let her know. "We can stop by the ranch and grab a shower and a change of clothes, and then I can head out to the prison before I go see Sunny."

She thought about the location of the prison, at least a thirty-minute drive, but it might be an hour round trip well spent while they were waiting on those test results. And at least if Jake went there, he wouldn't be risking arrest from the marshals.

"I can use the drive to the ranch to catch up on some phone calls," Jake added. "I want to ask Royce about Sunny and arrange to get some deputies from nearby towns to cover the station."

Yes, because Jake and she were obviously going to be tied up with this investigation. And hopefully, the bone marrow transplant for Sunny. She wasn't sure exactly what that entailed, but she didn't want Tanner's goons interfering with that.

"And we'll use the back roads to get from the ranch to the prison," he added.

"You think it's safe to go the ranch?" Maggie asked, though she would love a hot shower, as well.

"We won't stay long, and I'll make sure no one follows us. Plus, the ranch hands are still there, guarding the place." He stopped, stared at her. "When I visit with Tanner, it's probably a good idea if you wait here or at the police station in Amarillo."

Maggie didn't even have to think about her answer. "Not a chance." And she wouldn't back down on this. She would bargain with the devil again if it meant keeping Sunny and the rest of the McCalls safe.

"I'm going with you," she insisted.

And before Jake could argue about her decision, Maggie headed for the door.

Chapter Eleven

Jake was having second and third thoughts about this meeting with Tanner, but most of his concerns centered around Maggie. The entire time they'd been at the ranch for a quick breakfast and to shower and change, he'd tried to talk her out of coming with him.

Man, she was stubborn.

He hadn't forgotten that about her, but it wasn't a good time for that stubbornness to surface. He would have felt a lot easier about facing down Tanner if Maggie had been safely tucked away with the Amarillo P.D.

Of course, he wouldn't have stayed put while someone else asked the questions he wanted to ask. So, maybe they were both stubborn. Plus, the prison was the one place where Jake was sure Tanner couldn't attack them. Still, he didn't want to waste time here.

Jake had managed to call Royce and get an update on Sunny, but the rest of his planned calls had been a bust because of poor reception during the drive. Once they were back in Mustang Ridge and headed to Amarillo, he needed to finish up some business and arrange for duty relief for his deputy.

Maggie and he made their way through the security at the prison, and the guard led them to the visiting area where he seated them at the small table. Tanner wasn't there yet, but when he arrived, he'd be seated behind the thick glass.

That suited Jake just fine.

Tanner was certain to push a few of their buttons, and Jake didn't know if he could keep his temper in check, since Tanner had hired the triggerman who'd murdered Anna.

A muscle-bound man wearing a suit stood in the corner. Tanner's lawyer, Sherman Toliver. The guard had informed Maggie and Jake that he'd be there, probably to advise his client if the need arose. Judging from his glare, he didn't want this meeting to happen at all.

Beside him, Maggie drew in a deep breath and glanced around. Her nerves were definitely showing.

"There's still time for you to leave," Jake reminded her. "You can wait in the reception area with the security guard."

"No," she said before he even finished the offer. "I need to do this."

Yeah. He understood that.

Anna's death would always be a wound that wouldn't heal. For both of them. Jake could see that now, how Anna's death had crushed them both. But part of him still didn't want this shared kinship with Maggie. It would cause too many complications, not just for him but for his family.

Did that make him want her less?

No.

And that's why he reached out and slipped his hand over hers so he could give it a gentle squeeze. She looked at him, managed a slight smile, but it ended just as quickly as it came because the guard escorted Tanner to the table.

Tanner took one look at them and flashed an oily smile that put a knot in Jake's stomach.

The man hadn't changed much in the two years since

Jake had last seen him. Tall with a sturdy build. He no longer had a two-hundred-dollar haircut and that rich facade, but he still somehow managed to look formidable even in shackles.

Tanner sat, his attention fixed on Maggie, and he picked up the phone the same moment Jake did. Since there was no speaker function, Maggie moved closer to Jake so she could hear.

"Aww, I was hoping for Santa Claus," Tanner joked. "To what do I owe this special holiday visit?"

"You sent a message with Dr. Grange for us to see you so you could give us some important information," Jake fired back. "Information about the person you hired to kill us."

Tanner faked being surprised by gasping and widening his eyes. "Now, now, Sheriff McCall, you know I wouldn't do anything that heinous. And since this conversation is almost certainly being recorded, you also know I'd never say anything to incriminate myself."

"You're on death row," Maggie reminded him.

"But I do have appeals. Maybe even a pardon from the governor. A man's gotta think about that, huh?"

Tanner stood no chance of either, and Jake hoped his stare let the man know that.

Tanner leaned closer to the glass, met Jake's eyes. "But I don't think it would hurt matters to say how much I despise you. Both of you," he added, sparing Maggie a glance. "However, since you're alive, then I guess you managed to dodge any bullets that came your way. Too bad."

"Yeah. Your hired gun is now a DB."

Tanner just smiled. No way would he admit to hiring that gunman, so Jake went in a different direction. "David came to the ranch and said you two were no longer in each other's good graces."

The man's expression didn't change. "He's right. It appears David has grown a conscience or something."

Jake shook his head. "So, I'm to believe he's a changed man?"

"Believe what you will."

Maggie moved closer to the phone, which put her arm to arm with Jake. Tanner's attention went to that contact, and he lifted an eyebrow as if he sensed something between them.

"I heard rumors that you think your rift with David has something to do with me," Maggie tossed out there.

"It does," Tanner admitted. "Well, you and your dead sister. He heard word about the kid being sick, and David went all boo-hoo on me. Poor kid with no mom to save her life, and David believes that's my fault. A guilty conscience is the sign of a sick mind."

And in Tanner's own sick mind, that might actually make sense.

"David said it had something to do with a witness," Jake commented.

Tanner shrugged. "Maybe. And maybe David was just being disloyal to me. I mean, it's not as if I can walk out of here and take care of things myself. Some son," he grumbled.

"Does that mean you don't care if our deal is broken?" Maggie asked.

Tanner's anger was immediate, and it flashed like fire through his eyes. "Oh, I care all right." And even though that was all he said, it was a threat. "I'm sure you remember the terms of our deal that you broke. And you no doubt remember the consequences. You've already reneged on the part about staying away, but the consequences will be tenfold if you renege on the rest of it."

Jake silently cursed. That deal Maggie had made with

the marshals might cause Tanner to go after her with a vengeance. Of course, he was already trying to kill her, so maybe it couldn't get worse.

"Go ahead," Maggie said, her glare fixed to Tanner. "You know you're dying to tell me how much you want me dead."

She was trying to goad Tanner into saying something incriminating. Something that could be used against him in the appeals process.

But Tanner leaned back, chuckled. "You already know how I feel about you, Maggie. No need to spell it out."

There was some chatter behind them, and Jake looked back to see the guard escorting someone else into the room.

David.

Now, what the devil was he doing here? The lawyer, Sherman Toliver, must have wanted to know the same thing, because he made a beeline for them.

"What a treat." But Tanner didn't seem happy to see his son. Of course, it could be an act to make Jake believe there truly was a rift between David and him.

"Why are you here?" Maggie demanded.

David tipped his head to his father and moved closer to the phone. "He had one of his lawyers call and demand that I come. He said my visit could save Maggie's life."

Jake looked at Tanner to see his take on it, but he only shrugged. "I have no idea what he's talking about."

"You bastard." David's eyes narrowed to slits. "What kind of sick game are you playing now?"

"I could ask you the same thing." Tanner smiled when he looked at Maggie. "What do you think? Do you believe I'd give David any information that would save you or Jake?"

"No," she readily answered. "But I figure you're itching to brag about what you've done. For instance, you probably want us to hear why a man like Dr. Gavin Grange would possibly allow himself to be corrupted by a man like you."

Oh, Tanner got that smug look on his face, and again Jake had to rein in his temper. "Just speculating, of course, but most people can be corrupted for money. Not you and the good sheriff, of course. Apparently not my son, either. The only thing that can corrupt you is family and the quest for justice. How nauseating, right?"

"Nauseating is right," Maggie repeated sarcastically. "Are you saying you bought Grange?"

Tanner dismissed that with the wave of his hand.

"What about Wade Garfield?" Jake came out and asked when Tanner didn't add anything about Dr. Grange. "Is he working for you?"

"Wade," he repeated, the man's name curving his mouth into another smile. "He's some piece of work, huh? You were stupid to trust him."

Jake had known from the beginning. "He came to you after the project I did with him?"

"In a manner of speaking. If you expect me to tell you that I did business with him, then you're wrong."

"You're protecting him," David accused.

Tanner lifted his shoulder. "I'm protecting myself."

"You don't stand a chance of having your conviction overturned," Jake informed him. "The triggerman you hired rolled on you, Tanner. He had proof that you paid him. There's no way for you and your lawyers to get around that."

"As long as I have money, there are ways around everything."

Jake was afraid that was the truth, and it made him sick to his stomach to know that as long as Tanner drew breath, or had all that money, he would always be a threat. It wasn't what he wanted to do, but he might have to move Sunny and the rest of his family away from Mustang Ridge.

Away from their home.

But before things got that far, maybe he could figure out a way to stop Tanner once and for all.

Tanner turned back to Jake. "I'm surprised you haven't asked me about the details of your father's visit."

"It's on my to-do list," Jake said.

And yeah, he would ask his father all about it, but first he wanted to hear what Tanner had to say so he could compare his version against what Chet would tell him. Jake really wanted to trust his father on this, but he wasn't sure he could. However, he did know that his father would never do anything to endanger any of his kids or threaten Sunny's safety.

"I guess you know all about Chet's attempts to work out a deal with me to find Maggie," Tanner tossed out there.

No, he didn't know, and that's exactly the information Jake wanted. "What did my father supposedly offer you for the information?"

"In theory?" Tanner smiled again. "He offered me nothing, but I think he mentioned something about it being dangerous for Maggie to have her relocation identity revealed." He paused. "But what you really want to know—did Chet want me to kill Maggie after she donated the marrow to your precious daughter?"

"Did he?" And Jake hated that he even had to ask.

"What do you think?" Tanner laughed.

Jake was thinking he was glad the glass was between them or he would have punched this moron.

Maggie stood and latched on to Jake's shoulder. "We're wasting our time. He doesn't know how to tell the truth."

"Oh, I know how," Tanner insisted. "I know you should keep your eyes open. Even around my own son. I don't know what his angle is, but he's not playing for me right now."

"I'm trying to help them," David insisted. He leaned forward, his face close to the glass. "And if you send your dogs after me, remember that I have nearly as much money as you do. I can send dogs, too."

Jake watched Tanner's body language, to see if he could figure out if this rift was real. But he saw no verification of that. Tanner was practically beaming. A proud father. Maybe because his son was playing along with some plan that Tanner had concocted—get Maggie and him to trust David so that Tanner could use his son to dig the knife in a little deeper.

It wouldn't work.

Jake had no intention of trusting either of them.

David and Tanner held their stare a little longer, and then David walked out.

Jake turned back to Tanner, trying to figure out what he'd learned this visit, and he decided Maggie was right. It was a waste of time. He got up, ready to leave.

"About Dr. Grange," Tanner said. He waited until Jake was facing him again before he continued. "Why don't you check his banks accounts and see what you find? And I don't mean the accounts he has in name. Look in the ones he's set up for a certain charity organization."

Hell. That could be a bluff, but that smug look said otherwise. Jake made a mental note to do a financial check on the doctor.

Jake hurried now to get out of there and wished he had time for another shower. He felt as if he'd been mucking around in the dirt.

Maggie and he went back through security and into the main reception area where David appeared to be waiting for them.

"I came because I thought I would help you," David volunteered. "And if you think I'm lying, check phone records. My dad's lawyer called me a little over an hour and asked me to come."

A little over an hour ago was when Jake had phoned the prison to request a visit with Tanner. Maybe one of the prison officials had contacted the lawyer. Or maybe Tanner had managed to buy off one of those officials, too.

As long as I have money, there are ways around everything, Tanner had bragged, and Jake didn't think that was too far from the truth.

"One more thing," David said to them as they all walked toward the front door. He looked at Maggie. "I don't know what you plan to do with the evidence against me, but I'm begging you to destroy it."

That stopped Jake and her in their tracks. Maggie stared at him, shook her head. "Why would I do that?"

"Because I don't want it in my father's hands. You may not believe me, but he's trying to set me up for something. And with that evidence, he can send me to jail."

"Your father said he'd retaliate against me if I didn't hold to my bargain to keep the evidence from seeing the light of day. That doesn't sound like a man ready to use it against you."

"Then, you don't know him very well. I can tell you don't believe me, but he'll try to come after me, and he might do that with your evidence. Or God knows what else." David shook his head and walked away.

"What the heck was that about?" Maggie watched the man disappear into the parking lot.

"I don't know." In fact, this entire visit had been confusing and useless. Well, except for the part about Dr. Grange's finances.

That might give them some answers one way or another.

The moment they were back in the car, Jake called his deputy to get the number for an FBI friend, Special Agent Kade Ryland. Since it was Christmas Eve, Jake wasn't even sure the man would answer, but he thankfully did. Jake asked the agent to run a deep financial check on the doctor and his charities, and Kade assured him that he would.

"Any idea how long it will take to get that?" Maggie asked.

Jake started the engine and drove away, heading for the back roads. "No, but Christmas will probably slow things down." Most banks were already closed. However, there was one source of information that was available. "I need to talk to my father."

"Yes," she agreed. "But I don't think he'd cut a deal with Tanner."

"He hates you," Jake reminded her. Or at least, Chet hated Maggie's involvement in Anna's murder. His father wasn't very reasonable when it came to things like that.

Hell, neither was he, Jake had to admit.

"Chet wouldn't have sent a gunman after me. Not like that anyway. I hadn't even taken the bone marrow test yet."

True. Jake hated that was how he measured his father's innocence—in terms of the timing of that test. However, if the test had been completed and the marrow donated, then Jake would have to put his own father on their list of suspects.

His phone rang, and Jake saw his brother's number on the screen. "Royce?" he immediately answered.

Jake heard his brother say something, but he couldn't make out what because of the static. He checked the reception on his phone and had only two bars. He prayed they didn't go through a dead zone, and there were plenty of them in this rural part of the state.

"If you can hear me," he said to Royce, "we're on our way back from the prison visit."

"Good, because I need you to get here fast." That part came through loud and clear, but the next few words were garbled.

"Sunny's running a temperature," he finally heard Royce say. "It's not high, and the doctors say she's not in immediate danger, but she's asking for you."

God, no. The news hit Jake hard. A temp for most kids wasn't a big deal, but it could be for Sunny since she had a hard time fighting off infections.

Jake checked the time. "We can be there in about forty minutes." The only way to the hospital was back through Mustang Ridge, and Jake hit the accelerator. There was some snow on the country road, hopefully no ice, though, and there was zero traffic. Maybe that would allow him to get there faster.

Of course, faster wasn't nearly fast enough. Not with his little girl asking for him.

"I have good news, too," Royce said. There was another hiss of static that cut off the rest of what Royce was saying.

"What?" Jake practically yelled into the phone. Because heaven knew he could use some.

The static popped in and out. "You did it, Jake. We have a bone marrow match for Sunny."

Chapter Twelve

"Royce?" Maggie heard Jake repeat. He tried several more times, and with a stunned look in his face, he glanced at her. "We have a match for Sunny."

With all the bad going on, Maggie hadn't forgotten about the bone marrow tests, but the news still stunned her. Then, it filled her with an overwhelming sense of relief.

This would save Sunny.

The tears came, and she launched herself across the seat so she could give Jake a victory hug. He hooked his right arm around her, pulled her as close as she could get with the restraints of the seat belt, and Maggie could now hear the static on the phone.

"The match might be David," Jake said a heartbeat later. "Royce didn't get a chance to tell me if it was David or you."

Since she was Sunny's blood kin, Maggie had to believe it was her, but of course, there was the possibility it was David. If he'd actually taken the test, that is.

She eased back so she could meet Jake's gaze, and she saw the concern in the depths of his eyes.

Oh, mercy.

If the donor match was David, then he might use this in some sick way. Blackmail, maybe to get her to turn over the evidence against him that Maggie had already given to the marshals.

"It'll be you," Jake mumbled like a prayer. "Not David." He handed her the phone. "Try to get through to Royce."

Gladly. She found his number under Recent Calls and hit the Redial. Nothing. There wasn't enough of a signal for the call to go through.

"Try again in a mile or two when we're closer to town," he instructed.

Maggie glanced out at the landscape and spotted the red claystone ridges that gave the town of Mustang Ridge its name. They weren't far out at all, and that meant they wouldn't have to wait long for an answer.

Still, the seconds crawled by.

She tried the call to Royce again and was so focused on it that it surprised her when she heard Jake curse under his breath. Hoping that he hadn't thought of some other complication, she looked at him and saw that he had his attention on his rearview mirror. Maggie turned in the seat and saw the large pickup truck barreling up behind them.

"You have on your seat belt?" Jake asked.

That question got her heart pounding, and she glanced at the truck again. It was going way too fast for the road conditions.

"It's following us?" She checked to make sure her seat belt was secure. It was. Not only was the truck following them, it was getting closer—fast.

"I hope that's all it's doing. Get out the guns."

That didn't help her heartbeat or suddenly thin breath. Maggie threw open the glove compartment and took out the guns they'd put there before they'd gone into the prison to visit Tanner. She handed Jake his Colt and kept hold of the Smith & Wesson and the phone.

"Hell," Jake said. "Hold on."

Maggie glanced behind her again and saw how much closer the truck had gotten in the span of a few seconds. The driver had floored it, and it didn't appear he or she was moving out into the other lane to pass.

No.

It was coming right at them.

Maggie braced herself for the impact. And it came. Mercy, did it. The truck was much larger than their car, and when it slammed into them, the jolt snapped her forward.

Jake, too.

And she saw him fight to keep control of the car. He kept a firm grip on both the steering wheel and the Colt, but firm grips didn't do much when the truck rammed into them again. And again. The other driver was using them like a battering ram.

Jake tried to speed up, to stop another hit, but the truck sped up, as well.

Who the heck was doing this?

Tanner was no doubt behind it, but had he sent Dr. Grange, David or Wade after them? Or was this just another gun? If so, maybe Tanner had lured them to the meeting with this purpose in mind.

To send one of his killers after them.

Despite another jolt, Maggie looked behind them again, but this time she tried to see who was behind the wheel. The windshield was tinted, but she could make out two figures, and even though she could only see silhouettes, she thought the one in the passenger's seat was holding a rifle.

Oh, God.

"I'm pretty sure they're armed," she relayed to Jake. Which wasn't exactly a surprise since this was no doubt an attack. She didn't think this was the prank of a pair of drunks. No. Someone had planned this.

The truck plowed into them again, and there was the

sound of metal scraping on the asphalt, and Maggie saw their bumper go flying. Without that minimal protection between them, the truck jolted forward, not just ramming into them, but forcing them off the road.

Maggie said a quick prayer because there was no safe place for them to go. There was a mixture of huge boulders, mesquite trees and a ditch. And beyond that wasn't much better because of the steep red claystone and gypsum cliffs. They created a barrier that would keep Jake and her from getting far away from the shooter.

The tires on her side hit the ice and gravel mixture on the side of the road, and the car went into a skid. Jake gripped the steering wheel and tried to control the spin, but it was too late.

They hit the ditch.

It was like hitting a brick wall and was another fierce jolt that shook the entire car and them. They stopped with the vehicle's front end buried into the ditch, and the impact deployed the airbags. They burst out from the dash and smashed right into Jake and her.

Jake cursed and tried to bat away the bag so he could see. Maggie did the same, but she had no trouble seeing the truck because it was on her side of the car. It came to a stop on the road, and the driver jumped out.

No rifle, but he had a handgun. And he was a stranger. A hired gun, no doubt, because he used the truck for cover, and he took aim at Jake and her.

Maggie latched on to Jake to pull him down at the same moment he grabbed her. They pushed each other lower onto the seat. It wasn't a second too soon.

The bullet blasted through the passenger's-side window and sent a spray of safety glass right at them. The second bullet went through the now gaping space and slammed into the steering wheel.

Maggie's heart was past the pounding stage now, and she figured the next bullet could kill Jake or her. She lifted her hand, unable to see where she was aiming, and she fired off a shot. From the sound of it, she didn't hit anything, but maybe it would keep the shooter at bay while Jake or she could get into a better position to return fire.

If that was possible.

They were literally pinned down in a disabled car.

"This way," Jake said.

Staying low, he shoved open his door and pulled her out to the other side and onto the ground so that their car would give them some measure of protection. Good thing, too, because the next shot went into the seat where she'd just been.

Maggie managed to keep hold of both her gun and the phone, and while the bullets continued to come at her, she dialed 911. She heard the static, followed by a dispatcher's voice, and Maggie gave the person their location.

Maybe, just maybe, they would get backup before this gunman managed to kill them. Of course, what they might get was an innocent bystander. A holiday traveler, driving through what was normally a safe place. God knew what the gunman would do in a situation like that, because Maggie was betting he wouldn't leave any witnesses alive.

"We need to move," Jake told her the second she finished the call. "He's coming closer."

Maggie couldn't see the gunman, but the next shot he fired certainly seemed closer. They didn't have the ammunition to go round-to-round with this guy so their best bet was to get into a better position so they could take him out.

"He's not alone," Maggie reminded Jake. She slipped his phone into her coat pocket. "There's someone in the passenger's seat."

Maybe their suspect. She wanted to know the person's identity, but at the moment she was glad he was staying put.

One gunman at a time.

"We're moving over there." Jake tipped his head to a huge boulder. It was wide enough to shield them both but only about two feet high, which meant they'd have to continue to lie low. But the advantage—it wasn't that far away from the car.

Maggie nodded, took a deep breath and they dove behind it. The shots didn't stop, but thankfully they ricocheted right off the rock.

Unfortunately, they were still pinned down.

The shots stopped, and even though Maggie couldn't hear what was going on, she thought the gunman might be reloading. Jake lifted his gun and peered out from the side of the boulder. He barely had time to peek around it before the shots came right at him.

"Stay down," Maggie insisted, but she knew they had to do something to put an end to this.

"He reloaded faster than I thought he could," Jake said. Which meant this guy was a pro or else had brought multiple loaded weapons with him. Even if it was the latter, that still meant it would take him a second or two to switch out.

She looked behind them at the bluff and the clump of rocks and trees directly in front of it. The rocks were high enough so they wouldn't be forced to stay on their bellies. If they could get to that clump, they might have enough room to maneuver and be in a better position to return fire.

Of course, to get there, they'd have to risk being shot.

The next bullet convinced Maggie that it was a risk they'd have to take because the shooter was on the move again. Coming closer, and he would probably end up using their own car for cover so he could shoot them like fish in a barrel.

She glanced at Jake and saw that he, too, had his attention on the rock cluster. "Cover me. When I get there, I'll stop this SOB before he can get to you," he said.

Her cop's instincts kicked in. So did her feelings for Jake. Maggie didn't want him taking the bulk of the risks, and she didn't want him hurt. Plus, there was the other person in the truck. Whoever he was, he'd be armed and would no doubt come out shooting if Jake took out his comrade.

"We should go together," she whispered. "We could come out shooting and head for cover."

She saw the debate in his eyes, but it quickly ended when the shots came at them faster, practically nonstop.

"When he pauses again, let's go for it," Jake insisted.

Maggie waited, the sound of each shot slamming through her, and even though it seemed to take a lifetime or two, the bullets finally stopped. Jake and she didn't waste a second. With their guns ready and with Jake behind Maggie pushing her, they raced away from the boulder.

She fired a shot in the direction of the truck. Jake did, too, but she didn't think either of them hit anything. Running at full speed, they jumped behind the trees.

The ground was icy and slick, and Maggie's feet landed not on the ground as she'd expected but on a flat-surfaced rock that was just visible in the snow and dirt. Even though Jake had hold of her shoulder, she slipped out of his grip and kept right on slipping. She couldn't stop, couldn't control where she was going.

She fell hard onto the rocks, the side of her head striking a fallen tree limb. The pain was instant, blinding, and it knocked the breath out of her.

Jake latched on to her, trying to pull her behind cover. But it was too late. Maggie looked up and saw something she didn't want to see.

The gunman had his weapon aimed right at her.

JAKE KNEW HE DIDN'T have more than a second or two to stop Maggie from being killed, but the slick ground didn't give him a lot of control of his movements.

Since he hadn't had much luck pulling her behind one of the boulders, he dove at her, putting his body between the gunman and her. In the same motion, he pushed them back, away from the shooter, and Maggie and he went sliding down the embankment that separated the treed area from the claystone ridge.

They smacked into more rocks. Not good. Because Maggie's head was already bleeding, and he didn't want his attempt to save her to end up hurting even more than the gunman's bullet could have done.

The moment he got his footing, Jake pivoted and looked up, his gun ready to defend them. The shooter wasn't there. Too bad, because Jake would have had an easy shot to pick him off.

Beside him, Maggie groaned softly, and she struggled to get to her feet. Jake wanted to check and make sure she was okay, but it was too big a risk to take. If the gunman came to the top of that embankment, Jake needed to fire.

Using a boulder for support, Maggie got to an upright position, and she took aim. Her hand was shaky, but Jake didn't know if that was from the cold or some injury. Mercy, he hoped she was okay. He'd dragged her out of WITSEC, and even though he hadn't had a choice about that, he'd put her in direct danger not once but twice.

The seconds crawled by, and he tried to pick through the sounds of the winter wind battering the ridge and trees. He didn't hear footsteps, but that didn't mean the gunman and his partner weren't moving closer.

Maybe this time Jake would be able to take one of them alive so he could learn the identity of the person Tanner had hired. Or if it was indeed Tanner behind this. It was possible David was working a different angle from his father and had orchestrated these attacks. Maybe to get that evidence from Maggie. Or maybe just revenge.

There was a slight cracking sound on his left, and Jake pivoted in that direction. He saw the gunman dart behind one of the trees.

Hell.

Now the man had the high ground, and Maggie and he didn't have any way to take cover. They were trapped.

Without taking his attention off the tree, he used his left hand to motion for Maggie to watch the right side of the embankment. He didn't want to take out one of the gunmen only for Maggie and him to be ambushed by the other.

The waiting started again, and the adrenaline continued to slam through Jake. He was primed and ready for the fight, but he was afraid, too. If Maggie was indeed the bone marrow match for Sunny, then it was critical for him to keep Maggie alive.

But it was more than that.

He realized it was important for other reasons, too. She damn sure didn't deserve to die.

Finally, Jake saw the movement he'd been waiting for. It was just the edge of the gunman's coat sleeve. Jake didn't fire. He waited, knowing the guy would have to lean out from cover to get the shot.

But the guy didn't move.

Since Maggie was literally side by side with him, he felt her arm tense. That was the only warning Jake got before he saw the blurred motion from the corner of his eye.

Maggie fired.

Her hand was no longer shaking, and she double tapped the trigger. Jake still didn't take his focus off the man to his right, but he heard the sound of Maggie's bullets and knew she'd hit someone. Probably the second guy she'd spotted in the cab of that truck.

There was a groan of pain, and the sound of someone collapsing onto the ground.

The guy still standing behind the tree said something that Jake didn't catch, but Jake did recognize the next sound he heard.

Sirens.

They were still in the distance, but Maggie's 911 call had worked. Thank God. Backup was on the way.

The guy behind the tree turned and started running. No doubt to get back to the truck. Jake couldn't let that happen. He needed at least one of these SOBs alive so he could get those answers they desperately needed. If not, the attacks would just continue.

"Cover me," Jake said to Maggie, and he latched on to the rocks to hoist himself to higher ground.

It wasn't easy, and he slipped a few times, but Jake finally made it to the top.

And he cursed.

He caught just a glimpse of the second gunman as the guy jumped into the truck. Before Jake could even take aim or get a good look at him, he sped away in the opposite direction of those sirens.

Jake ran so he could try to get a look at the license plate, but it was coated with mud or something. Probably on purpose so the vehicle couldn't be traced. Still, he had a description, and maybe the second gunman had some kind of identification on him that would lead him back to Tanner or one of their suspects.

Jake's gaze shifted to the downed gunman. The guy wasn't moving, and he needed to check for any signs of life. First, though, he checked on Maggie. She was pale, and there was blood trickling down the left side of her face. She also had bruises and scrapes, but he hoped her injuries weren't serious.

He helped her up the embankment, and they reached the top just as a police cruiser pulled to a stop. Thankfully, Jake recognized the man—it was Shawn Marcus, the sheriff of Corral Junction, a town just ten miles or so from Mustang Ridge. They not only knew each other, they'd worked together.

"You all right, Jake?" Shawn called out. He had his weapon drawn.

"Two men attacked us." Jake let go of Maggie's hand, and he hurried to the downed gunman. He touched his fingers to the guy's neck. No pulse.

Later, Jake would send someone back to collect the body and any evidence, but for now he latched on to Maggie again and raced toward Shawn.

"The second gunman got away, and he's headed east toward Corral Junction," Jake explained. "We need to stop him." And find out who he was.

The three of them didn't waste any time getting into Shawn's cruiser, and the sheriff drove out of there fast. "I'm the only one on duty today," he explained. "I gave the deputies the day off."

And that meant there wasn't anyone immediately available to set up a roadblock. Not in time anyway. At the speed the truck had been going, the driver would be in town in just a minute or two.

Jake gave Shawn a description of the vehicle, and the sheriff radioed in the information. Maybe they'd get lucky and some off-duty officer could stop the vehicle. Jake used the cruiser's CB to contact his own deputy and alert him. Of course, the gunman could turn off on one of the farm roads between the two towns and meander his way to a main highway.

In other words, they might not catch him.

Jake pushed that possibility aside and turned to Maggie, who was in the backseat. He took a wad of tissues from the box between the two front seats and he leaned over so he could dab the blood and see how deep the cut was.

"I'm okay," she mumbled.

That was a big lie, but he didn't want to call her on it because Maggie was barely managing to hold herself together. That was almost certainly the first person she'd ever killed, maybe the first she'd ever shot, and he knew from experience that it would hit her hard.

"I need to call Royce," Jake said, and he reached out for his phone, which she'd put in her pocket.

She shook her head. "Don't tell him about this."

"I won't." Not over the phone anyway. That could wait until they were face-to-face at the hospital. There'd be plenty of time for talk then, and while there, Maggie could get the checkup she needed for her injuries.

Maggie took over holding the tissues and pressed them to her wound while she handed him the phone. Jake was about to punch in Royce's number, but it rang before he could do that.

"Jake, it's me, Kade. I got a quick answer for you on those financials you requested."

The money trail for Dr. Grange. Jake certainly hadn't expected anything so soon.

"There's a boatload of recently deposited funds in one of Grange's accounts," Kade explained. "And there's no logical paper trail to justify those funds. They were placed into his account via a wire transfer. Not a direct one, either. The funds bounced around among servers and dummy companies so it'll make it hard to trace the source."

Jake was torn between relief and anger. Grange was

someone he trusted, and the cash could be a giant red flag that the doctor had sold out to Tanner.

"You found it so fast," Jake speculated, "that I have to wonder if it wasn't planted."

"Maybe, but it was Grange or someone with direct access to his personal account who made the final transfer. It looks as if he tried to hide the funds in an account he set up for a charity foundation to provide counseling and rehab to troubled teens. You might remember that Grange's own son was an addict and committed suicide about five years ago, and that's why Grange set up the charity."

Jake did remember the suicide and the circumstances surrounding it. And it was an admirable charity, but funneling funds into it didn't sound like the actions of an innocent man. Unless Tanner's hired goons had somehow manipulated the paperwork.

Jake thanked Kade for the information, and the moment he ended the call, the text from Royce popped up on the screen.

There's been a bomb threat at the hospital. Get here NOW.

Chapter Thirteen

Maggie's heart was beating way too fast. Her breath was gusting. But she couldn't make herself calm down. Not with Sunny at risk.

Shawn Marcus, the Corral Junction sheriff, brought his cruiser to a squealing stop directly in front of the Amarillo hospital. There were uniformed officers all around. A bomb squad truck, too.

Once they'd made it out of the dead zone, Jake had managed to speak briefly with Royce so Jake and she knew the area had been contained, that there didn't appear to be any gunmen present, just the threat of the bomb, but the threat was enough to get Sunny evacuated. Evacuated where, though, Jake and she didn't know.

"I'm Sheriff Jake McCall," he shouted as he barreled from the cruiser.

One of the uniforms nodded and motioned for them to follow him. Jake said a quick goodbye and thanks to his fellow sheriff, and Maggie and he began to run.

The adrenaline was knifing through her, and there was nothing left of her composure by the time they made it to the back parking lot of the building where there were several ambulances. More uniformed officers, too. They went straight to the one where both Royce and Chet were standing. The men had their guns drawn and were keeping watch.

"Sunny's okay," Royce immediately volunteered, and he tipped his head to the ambulance. "Nell and the nurse are in there with her. And the bomb threat was just that. A threat. They took the dogs through there, and they found nothing."

Maggie allowed herself a short breath of relief, but she knew she wouldn't feel even marginally better until she saw Sunny's face.

Royce glanced at Maggie's head. "What about you two? Were you hurt?"

"No," Maggie said, but then Jake wiped at the cut on the side of her head. It was such a minor injury compared to what could have happened. "I'm just anxious to see Sunny."

Jake must have felt the same way because he reached for the rear ambulance door.

"By the way," Royce said, catching on to his brother's arm. His gaze shifted to Maggie. "You're the bone marrow match for Sunny."

That robbed Maggie of what little breath she had, and the tears sprang to her eyes. Happy tears, this time. Well, happy until she remembered the danger they were still facing. Jake and she had just come close to dying. Maybe Sunny would have, too, if this had been a real bomb threat. It wouldn't do much good if she saved Sunny with the bone marrow, only to have them dropped right back into danger.

"You're going through with the donation, right?" Chet asked, and as usual his tone was a bark without a trace of friendliness.

Maggie didn't mind the bark so much. She deserved it, but she had to wonder what Chet would say about his meeting with Tanner. Now wasn't the time to ask about that, but she doubted Jake would put it off for long. They needed answers, and unfortunately, Chet might have them.

"Of course I'm going through with it," Maggie assured him, and she looked at Jake to see how he was dealing with this.

Like her, there was relief in his eyes. Worry, too. And there was the underlying fear that even though she was a match, she had to stay alive to save Sunny.

Royce's expression was considerably kinder than his father's when he looked at Maggie. "As soon as this bomb threat is lifted and we've made arrangements to move Sunny to a new location, I'll start the plans for the marrow donation."

She nodded, mumbled a thanks and wiped away the tears when Jake opened the ambulance door. Maggie didn't want Sunny to see her crying.

Jake and she stepped into the ambulance, and Maggie met Nell's gaze first. Yet another concerned McCall. Sunny was on the small gurney, the covers on her and an IV still attached to her arm.

She opened her eyes and smiled at them.

It was weak, but it warmed Maggie from head to toe.

"Glad you're here," Nell whispered to both of them. She reached out, gave Maggie's hand a squeeze. "I'll give you guys some time alone."

Nell stepped out of the ambulance and thankfully so did the nurse. Maggie didn't know how much time they would have, but she wanted to make every minute count. Then, she'd need to give Jake some alone daddy-daughter time, too.

Jake took some of the antiseptic wipes from the shelf next to the gurney, and he wiped his hands before giving one to Maggie for her to do the same.

"You came," Sunny said, her attention shifting back and forth between them.

"Of course we did." Jake ran his fingers through her hair, kissed her forehead. "How are you feeling, baby?"

She yawned, wiped her eyes. "My head hurted a little, but it's better now."

Probably a headache from the fever. It was yet another reminder of just how sick her precious niece was.

Sunny took Maggie's hand and urged her closer to the gurney so that Jake and she were kneeling side by side next to the little girl.

"Does your head hurted, too?" Sunny asked, looking at Maggie's cut.

"No," Maggie assured her.

But Sunny didn't seem to believe that. She also looked at the scratch on the back of her daddy's hand and then the mud on both their jackets.

"We slipped and fell down," Jake said before Sunny could ask. "We're clumsy, huh?"

That brought back the smile. "Aunt Nell says you're gonna make me all better now," she said to Maggie.

"I am." And Maggie wasn't going to allow any room for doubt. This had to work.

"I'll maybe feel good soon," Sunny added in a whisper. She turned back to Jake, and the smile vanished. "Santa might not find me here."

"You'll get your presents, baby," Jake promised. The emotion weighed down his voice, but Maggie could tell he was trying to hide his concerns from his daughter. "One of the ranch hands can get them from Santa and bring them to you."

"But what about the other present?" Sunny asked, staring at Maggie. "I want you to come live with us and be my mommy."

Oh, mercy. Maggie hadn't wanted to tackle this today. "Let's talk about that after Christmas."

The skeptical look returned. It was much too perceptive for a child so young. "That means you're gonna say no. 'Cause that's what Daddy says when he doesn't want to say no right off."

"It's not a no," Maggie assured her. She was digging herself into a deep hole. "I just don't know what my plans are yet."

Well, other than doing the bone marrow donation and then going to WITSEC. But even that might be out. She certainly didn't want to start a new life as someone else if Sunny and the rest of the McCalls weren't safe. And the only way for that to happen was to get Tanner and his lackeys out of the picture. If by some miracle that happened then she wouldn't need WITSEC, and the McCalls wouldn't need protecting.

Sunny held up her index finger and blew on it as if it were a candle. "It's like a wish," she whispered. "If we all do it, it might come true."

Maggie glanced at Jake and figured the discomfort she saw there on his face pretty much matched the uneasiness on hers. Still, Sunny was clearly waiting, so Maggie blew on the tip of her index finger.

"Your daddy probably needs to save his wishes for other things," Maggie suggested so she could give Jake an out. Despite their recent *closeness,* there was no way he'd want her at the ranch.

But Sunny just kept staring at him, just kept waiting, until Jake finally blew at his finger, too.

Sunny clapped her hands, but that seemed to sap the rest of her energy. She yawned again. "Merry Christmas, Daddy," she whispered. "Merry Christmas, Aunt Maggie."

Jake kissed her again. Maggie leaned over and did the

same. As much as she wanted to stay there and not lose a moment with Sunny, there were things that had to be done. Like the preparations for the bone marrow donations.

But first and foremost, they had to keep Sunny safe.

Jake and she stepped from the ambulance, and Nell and the nurse immediately went back in. Royce was talking on the phone, so that left Maggie facing Chet.

"Tanner said you visited him in prison," Jake said, taking the words out of her mouth. "He claims you tried to cut a deal with him."

Chet's eyes narrowed, but what he didn't do was deny it. "I thought he knew where Maggie was."

God. It was true. Tanner hadn't lied about that—Chet had visited him.

Jake huffed. "And if he did, you believed he'd just give you this information for nothing?"

"No." Chet's mouth tightened, he repeated it and glanced away. "I figured Tanner would make me pay somehow."

"With Maggie's death?" Jake questioned.

"No!" And that time, Chet didn't hesitate. "Look, there's no goodwill between me and her, but her death would have solved nothing. Just the opposite. We need her alive for Sunny."

"She's helping all of us," Jake corrected. "Maggie's put her neck on the line, and what I want to know is if you made it worse by going to Tanner. Did he ask you to kill Maggie? I don't mean before she found out she was a match but did he want you to kill her after she donated the bone marrow?"

Chet opened his mouth, closed it, opened it again and looked as if he were ready to pitch a fit. But the fit of temper came and went, and he groaned and scrubbed his hand over his face. "Tanner made that offer. I turned it down."

"Did you?" Maggie pressed, and she hated that she even had to ask.

She braced herself for a tongue-lashing for questioning Chet's innocence, but he looked her straight in the eye. "I turned him down," he repeated. "But he let me know he'd just hire somebody else."

Now it was Jake's turn to groan. "According to David, Tanner didn't hire anyone to kill Maggie. He hired someone to kill me."

The color blanched from Chet's weathered face. "David could be lying." But he didn't sound any more convinced of that than Maggie was.

Jake stared at his father. "If you know anything about Tanner's plans—"

"I don't," Chet insisted. "And I sure as hell wouldn't have sat there and listened to him go on about hiring someone to kill my son." He glanced at Maggie's cut and Jake's hand. "Is that what happened to you? You ran into Tanner's hired gun?"

"Probably." Jake wearily shook his head. "But now we need to find out who Tanner hired."

Chet didn't have time to speculate on that because Royce finished his call and stepped closer. "I want to move Sunny to another hospital here in town." He put his hands on his hips and glanced at both of them. "How do you two feel about creating a diversion so that we can make sure no one follows Sunny?"

"What do you have in mind?" Jake asked.

"It's risky, but if any of Tanner's men are around here, maybe you can lead them somewhere else?"

Jake looked at her, waited for Maggie to nod. "Give us the keys to your SUV. The rest of you can ride in the ambulance with Sunny. Get some plainclothes officers to go with you."

Yeah, it was risky, for Jake and her, but it sounded as if he was making this as safe as possible for Sunny.

"What about the bone marrow donation?" Maggie asked. "When and where?"

"Around midnight." He checked his watch. "About ten hours from now. It's the best I could do." Royce paused. "And it'll be done at the small hospital in Corral Junction. Betsy Becker will meet you there about a half hour prior and will sneak you in through the back."

Betsy, Sunny's nurse, had given them no reason not to trust her. Maggie hoped that continued.

"Betsy's helping with the donation, too. Her cousin's a doctor, and he's done these procedures before. She's convinced him to come to the hospital and do it. It'll be very hush-hush, and hopefully you can be out in no time. There'll be minimal staff because of Christmas, so maybe we can keep this from getting back to Tanner."

None of them said anything right away. They stood there, trying to absorb it all.

"What then?" Chet asked. "We all just can't go walking around free as birds?"

"No," Royce agreed. "If we can't deal with Tanner once and for all, we're all going to need to disappear."

"WITSEC?" Chet practically howled.

"Or something like it," Royce clarified. "Maggie, Jake and Sunny could go alone, but Tanner would just try to use Nell, you and me to draw Jake right back out."

Oh, God. Royce was right.

This could cost the McCalls their ranch. Their home. Their lives.

"One thing at a time," Jake reminded them. "Let's take care of Sunny, and we'll go from there."

"I agree. I need to call the other hospital and let them know we're coming. I'll make sure they keep our arrival a secret." Royce took his SUV keys from his pocket and handed them to Jake. He motioned to the space where he'd parked. "Will you two be taking any more trips to where there's bad phone reception?"

"No," Jake assured him. "I'm taking Maggie to the ranch."

Both Chet and Royce looked at him as if he'd lost his mind.

"Not to the house," Jake said. "But to one of the out-buildings."

That could mean anything from a barn to one of the ranch hands' cabins. It probably wouldn't be comfortable, or warm, but it was only for a few hours until they had to leave for the hospital.

Another place that would be hard to secure.

Maggie hoped the procedure could be done quickly so Jake and she could get in and out.

"Use my house," Royce offered. "It has a security system."

And it was on the grounds of the ranch. Small, if she remembered correctly, but better than a barn.

"If things don't go well," Jake said to his brother, "call one of the ranch hands and have them bring Sunny's presents to whatever hospital you're at."

Royce huffed. "I will, but Sunny's not going to like that. She'll want you there come Christmas morning."

"I know." And Jake repeated it under his breath. "I'll do everything humanly possible to make that happen."

He would. No one there doubted that, but there were a lot of things that Tanner could throw at them.

Maggie looked at Jake, snagged his gaze. "Once you have the bone marrow, you'll leave and come back here to be with Sunny."

"You'll be sedated," he reminded her. "In no shape for me to leave."

"Yes, I will be. You're spending Christmas with Sunny."

Jake looked as if he wanted to argue with that. And then as if he didn't. But as far as Maggie was concerned, there was nothing to argue about.

"We'll wait in the parking lot until you drive away," Jake finally said to Royce. "And then we'll leave. If Tanner has a man in place near here, we'll make sure he sees us. I want him following us, not you."

Jake said goodbye to his brother and dad, and while they were making their way across the parking lot, his phone rang. "It's Billy," he relayed to her.

Maggie hoped the deputy wasn't calling with bad news. They'd already had enough of that for the day. For an entire lifetime.

Jake and she got into the SUV, but he didn't start the engine. "Why does he want to talk to me?" Jake asked Billy. He paused. "Give him this number."

The moment Jake finished his call with Billy, he looked at her. "Dr. Grange is going to call in a few minutes."

Maggie wasn't exactly surprised when she heard the identity of the caller. After all, Grange was a suspect, and he knew it. Maybe the doctor had heard about their visit to the prison. Or worse. Maybe he'd been the person who had fled in the truck after firing shots at them.

She scooted closer to him so she could hear, and she waited. It was the first moments of silence they'd had, well, since the cabin. Not exactly silence, though, since her thoughts had been going a mile a minute.

Still were.

Jake had that effect on her.

Maggie looked at him at the exact moment he looked at her. They glanced away as if they'd been caught doing something wrong. And before she could stop herself, she laughed. It wasn't funny. Nothing about their situation was, but the awkwardness between them was almost palpable.

The heat, too.

The corner of his mouth lifted. A killer dimple flashed in his cheek. "We're a pair, aren't we? Our baggage has got baggage." His tone was light, but the smile didn't stay. Nor did the eye contact. He glanced at the ambulance and Royce, who was still on his phone, no doubt making arrangements for Sunny's transfer to another hospital.

She couldn't argue with him or the crazy intimacy going on between them. "I think I'm falling for you," Maggie confessed. It was probably stupid, but if she was going to die, she was at least going to get that off her chest.

"Don't," he warned. But then Jake leaned in and brushed his mouth over hers. His lips were rough from the cold and wind, and even though the gesture was gentle, he wasn't. The pressure deepened. So did the grip he put on her arm to urge her closer.

"And that's your answer to don't?" she asked.

He shook his head, checked the ambulance again. "No. That was me making a mistake."

She ran her tongue over her bottom lip and tasted him there. "It didn't feel like a mistake."

"It never did between us. And that was part of the problem."

They were talking about the kiss in the barn now. Ancient history. Or maybe not, she decided, when he kissed her again.

What were they talking about?

One thing was for sure—she needed to keep her head, because the man and his kisses were getting to her. How could just a touch from his lips start that kind of fire inside her? Jake's kisses simmered through her. Her mouth. Her breasts. Her belly.

And lower.

All with a kiss that Jake considered a mistake.

The sound shot through the SUV, and Maggie embarrassed herself by gasping. It was just the phone, something they'd been expecting. Something the kiss had caused her to forget. "Sheriff McCall," Dr. Grange said crisply when Jake answered. "Tanner's lawyer just phoned me with a heads-up that you're having my financials investigated."

"I am." Jake glanced at her, cleared his throat and stared at the ambulance. "And there's suspicious money in one of your accounts," he added. "Care to tell me how it got there?"

"I didn't put it there, but my guess is Tanner did, to make me look guilty. Judging from the tone of your voice, he succeeded."

"Haven't made up my mind about that yet. I just want to know the truth. I'm tired of getting shot at, tired of nearly getting Maggie killed, and I'm especially tired of the fact that something about your situation with Tanner just doesn't add up. Now, tell me, what doesn't add up?"

It was several seconds before Grange said anything. "Tanner's blackmailing me. Not for money. But he's got something he keeps holding over my head."

Maggie certainly hadn't expected to hear the doctor say that, and she moved even closer to Jake so she wouldn't miss a word of the explanation. She also checked on the ambulance. Still there.

"I'm listening," Jake prompted.

Grange's breath was loud enough for Maggie to hear it. "Three years ago, I was looking for land to build an outpatient drug rehab center for my charity foundation, and Tanner owned a property I started researching." He paused again. "I found out the land hadn't exactly been obtained legally."

Oh, no. Maggie suddenly got a really bad feeling about this. *Please*. Don't let this go where she thought it might be going.

"What did you do?" Jake pressed.

"Look," the doctor said, "the only reason I didn't tell you is because of Chet. You know his temper. And I thought he might try to ruin me. Or kill me."

"Oh, mercy." Maggie groaned. It was about *that*. She hadn't known that Grange had been the one to start it, but she knew it now.

And Jake was about to know it, as well.

"What the hell are you talking about?" Jake asked.

Maggie wanted to scream, to pull the phone from Jake's ear, but Pandora's box had already been opened.

"When I found the suspicious land deal," the doctor explained, "I told someone. Someone I wanted to take the information to the cops. I didn't want Tanner to know I'd been the one to find it, and I told this *someone* not to mention my name to the cops."

Beside her, Jake went perfectly still. "Who's the *someone*?" he asked.

And Maggie knew she had to be the one to tell him. Not that it would be easier coming from her. No. It would only reopen old wounds just starting to heal. Still, he had to hear it from her.

"Jake, it was Anna," Maggie whispered.

Chapter Fourteen

Jake was glad he was sitting down.

Glad, too, that he didn't have to respond immediately to either Dr. Grange or Maggie. That's because he saw Royce motion to him, and his father got into the back of the ambulance. Royce jumped into the front passenger's seat. The driver pulled out of the parking lot, and Jake knew he would have to put his emotions and the conversation on the back burner.

Sunny's safety came first.

He pressed the end-call button, and he drove out behind the ambulance. It went right. Jake went left, and he braked to a loud stop directly in front of two uniformed officers.

Jake lowered his window. Maggie did the same. And Jake asked a question about the bomb. Still no sign of one, the officer reported. Just as Jake had expected. But the question was meant for anyone waiting and watching. Jake wanted the person to see Maggie and him and follow them instead of going after the ambulance with Sunny inside.

Of course, there was a chance one of Tanner's goons would try to follow the ambulance as well, but Royce would be looking for that. His brother wouldn't allow the ambulance to stop at the hospital until he was sure it was safe.

It was good to have family to watch his back.

And the brief thought that flashed through his head brought other thoughts with it. Of Anna. *God.*

Maggie took her gun from her coat pocket and turned in the seat to keep watch. Jake put the phone on the seat so he could do the same. He drove away from the hospital and caught just a glimpse of the ambulance as it disappeared over a hill. Jake headed for the highway that would take Maggie and him back to Mustang Ridge.

"Is it true?" Jake asked her. Yeah, the timing for the question sucked, but he'd never had good timing with Maggie.

"Yes."

Her voice was a whisper, but Jake heard it as clearly as if she'd shouted. There it was again. That punch of grief that always came with thoughts of Anna.

The punch of guilt, too.

"I didn't know it was Grange who found the land record." Her voice stayed a whisper. "Anna didn't tell me that. But she brought the land file to me and asked me to take a look at it because she thought something illegal had gone on."

Another punch. This one was mixed with hurt and confusion. "Why the hell didn't she come to me?"

Maggie didn't take her attention off their surroundings. "You're sure you want to know the truth, Jake? Because you're not going to want to hear it."

That didn't ease the knot in his stomach or the pressure in his chest. "Tell me," he demanded.

She glanced at him, and he saw sorrow in her eyes.

"Chet sold that land to Tanner," she said. "And yes, they made some kind of deal, because Chet got paid triple the value of the property and then turned around and bought another piece of land from Tanner using the cash from the first deal."

Jake mentally went through all that. "Are you saying my father and Tanner used the land to launder money or something?"

"Yes. I think Chet was a very small cog in what turned out to be a big money-laundering scheme, but Anna didn't want you to have to bring your father in for questioning."

"Or arrest him," Jake finished for her.

Maggie nodded. "Nell didn't know," she added. "Nor Royce. Your father hid the land deal from all of you, and he might not have even realized it was illegal. Tanner could have put a spin on it to make it all sound legit."

"Why didn't *you* arrest my father?" Jake snapped.

"Because Anna begged me not to. She didn't want you hurt. And besides, I found other land deals much worse than the one Tanner did with Chet. I had more than enough evidence and witnesses to send Tanner to jail even before his murder conviction."

Jake had to remind himself to breathe, and he took a moment before he tried to speak. "Tanner found out that Anna had cued you into the investigation?"

She nodded. "I'm not sure how, but after the fact...after we learned Tanner was the one who had her murdered, he told me that he knew."

"Someone told him?" Jake pressed.

"I don't think so. I think Tanner's people just put one and one together since Anna worked at the land office."

Yeah. That wouldn't have been a long leap for Tanner to make.

"I didn't use that land deal with Chet in any of my investigation reports," Maggie added. "Yes, I withheld evidence, but I thought it was for a good reason. Justice wouldn't have been served putting Chet in jail. Plus, I rationalized that I could always classify him as a material witness if I needed additional testimony against Tanner.

"There's more," Maggie said after a long pause. "Anna also gave me the evidence I have against David. In fact, Anna's the one who signed those documents."

He cursed, and it was bad. "Are you saying Anna did something illegal?"

"No," she quickly assured him. "I think she was just fooled, that David had altered the paperwork so Anna didn't know until after the fact that something was wrong."

With all of that flying through his head, Jake took the highway toward Mustang Ridge. There was still no sign of anyone following them so he passed his phone to Maggie.

"This conversation isn't over," he said, "but I need to make sure no one is following the ambulance. Call Royce."

Maggie pressed in the numbers that Jake gave her. "Is everything okay?" she asked when Royce answered.

Jake didn't have to hear his brother's answer to know all was well. He could tell from Maggie's body language. She loosened the death grip she had on the phone. A short breath left her mouth.

"No one's following them," Maggie relayed to him, and put the phone back on the seat. But her relieved body language didn't last.

Probably because she knew what he was about to ask.

"When Anna was killed, did you suspect Tanner?"

"No. If I had, I would have told you." She shook her head, groaned softly. "Like you, I thought Anna was just a victim of a robbery gone bad. I didn't connect it to Tanner because I didn't think he knew about Anna bringing me that land file. And I certainly didn't think he'd go after her to get back at me."

"Tanner threatened you, though," Jake reminded her.

"*Me*. Not Anna. Not anyone else. I figured it was a bluff. After all, there was no proof he'd ever killed anyone, and those initial charges wouldn't have given him life in prison.

In fact, with his lawyers, he probably could have cut a deal and gotten just a few years behind bars."

Apparently, Tanner's fury over the investigation had robbed him of his common sense. And it'd robbed Jake of Anna.

"Why didn't you tell me that Anna wanted you to do the investigation?" he asked.

"I thought you had enough to deal with without adding that. Besides, it didn't matter. Anna was dead."

"It mattered," he let her know. "I put the blame for her death on you."

"That's where it belongs."

"No. Hell, it doesn't even belong on my father." Though Jake did want to know why Chet hadn't volunteered any of his part in the Tanner investigation. "Nor Anna. All the blame is on Tanner."

Maggie made a small *hmm* sound. Possibly of agreement. "Did we just reach some kind of understanding here?" But she waved him off before he could answer. "No. That would minimize what happened. I don't want to do that."

"Not minimize," Jake corrected. "But maybe we can get to a place where we aren't hurting each other."

The next sound was of humor. Also small. "Does that have something to do with us kissing?"

"It'd be easier if it did," Jake remarked, and he left it at that.

He turned onto the farm road that would lead to the ranch. Eventually. He still wanted to do some meandering to make sure no one was following them, but at the moment there wasn't another car in sight. Probably because it was late afternoon on Christmas Eve. Most people were already tucked inside with their families, getting ready for the big celebration.

Jake envied them.

Normal was something he hadn't had in a long time, and after glancing at Maggie, he wondered if he'd ever have it again.

His phone rang, and Jake snatched it up, praying that all was still well with Sunny and the others. But it was his deputy, Billy.

"Wade Garfield wants to talk to you right away," Billy relayed. "He said it was important, but I didn't want to give your number until I'd talked with you."

Wade. Just somebody else to add to his weariness and frustration. "Did Wade tell you what was so important that he had to talk to me right away?"

"I asked, but he wouldn't say. He sounded scared, or something."

Probably the *or something*. "Give him the number," Jake said, and he hung up so Wade could make his call, which would no doubt turn out to be another frustrating experience.

"Is Wade still claiming someone's trying to kill him?" Maggie asked, her voice dripping with sarcasm.

"Probably. Or maybe he wants to put another tracking device on a vehicle I'm driving."

The phone rang, and even though it was a call he dreaded, Jake answered it.

"Sheriff McCall," Wade said the second Jake answered, "I have to see you right away."

Jake ignored that. "What do you want?"

"To meet with you. Didn't you hear me? I have something important to tell you."

That seemed to be the trend of the day. Tanner, Dr. Grange, now Wade. David was the only one of their suspects not clamoring to see him.

"If it's that important," Jake said, "you can tell me over the phone."

"No," Wade insisted after a few seconds. "We have to do this face-to-face. I won't have you recording the conversation so you can use it against me."

"Sheez. Paranoid much? Wade, the only time I'd use a conversation against you is if you've committed a crime. Like, say, trying to kill us. Where were you about an hour ago?"

"I'd rather not discuss that. In fact, I'd rather not tell anyone where I am."

"Yeah, yeah. Because someone wants you dead. Welcome to the club."

"Are you accusing me of something?" Wade asked.

"Are you guilty of something?" Jake countered.

That caused Wade to curse. "Look, if you want what I have, then you have to meet me. But I think you should know, I figured out a way to stop Tanner for good."

"How?" Jake demanded.

But he was talking to himself, because Wade had already hung up.

MAGGIE LOOKED OUT THE living room window at the snow that had just started to fall. A white Christmas. Well, a white Christmas Eve anyway, but it would likely stick through the following day.

Too bad the following day came with so many uncertainties.

Behind her, Jake paced while he spoke on the phone, something he'd been doing since they arrived an hour earlier. He'd even fixed sandwiches for both of them and eaten one while checking on Sunny and getting updates on the investigation. That was good, because Maggie needed some time to think. So far, she'd failed at that, but at least his nonstop calls had prevented her from blurting out all her fears.

Jake had enough to handle.

She glanced at him, intending a quick look to gauge his mood so he could figure out if he was getting good or bad news from the caller. But in that split-second glance, their gazes met, and he came closer, looking out the window from over her shoulder. Maybe to verify that she hadn't seen anything unsettling.

But the only unsettling thing was Jake.

He ran his hand down her arm, and he leaned in, his chest against her back. She drew in his scent. Felt his heart beating. His breath, on her neck. Even his words seemed to vibrate against his skin.

"Snow," he whispered to her and brushed an idle kiss on her cheek.

Her heart did a little flip-flop. It was the kind of affectionate gesture that seemed second nature for most. Certainly not for her, and she wondered if a simple touch from him could ever feel routine. She did a gut check and decided the answer was no.

Jake wasn't a routine kind of guy.

"That was Sheriff Shawn Marcus," he relayed to her when he finished the call. He also stepped away to look at the laptop he'd placed on the breakfast bar that divided the living room from the kitchen. "There was no ID on the body of the man who tried to kill us, but Shawn got a match on his fingerprints."

That was a hopeful-sounding bit of information. "Who was he?"

"His name was Simpson Carter. He has a long criminal record, and Shawn's trying to see if there's a money trail to connect him to the person who hired him. Special Agent Kade Ryland is helping with that."

"But?" she asked when he flexed his eyebrows.

"But because of the holidays, we might not get a quick answer. Certainly not before you have the procedure done in Corral Junction."

So, they still weren't any closer to stopping Tanner. Unless... "What about Wade?" she asked. "You think he really knows how to stop Tanner?"

He lifted his shoulder. "I've tried to call him back twice, but they've both gone directly to voice mail."

That didn't sound promising. Maybe Wade was just playing a game so they might jump at the next chance to meet with him. Or he could be hurt. Or worse. After all, Wade had insisted that Tanner or someone else was trying to kill him.

"Billy's trying to find him," Jake added, probably because he hadn't dismissed Wade's accusations against Tanner, either. "When the procedure's done and Sunny is recovering, I can look at other ways to tackle Tanner."

"Maybe with David's arrest," she suggested. Maggie turned to stare out the window again. "We could possibly use the charges against him to freeze his assets. Maybe freeze his father's assets, too." It wasn't something just off the top of her head. Maggie had been going through all their less-than-stellar options.

Jake nodded and scrolled through something on the laptop screen. "Cutting off Tanner's money supply would put an end to his hired guns." He paused, looked up at her. "Anything wrong out there?"

Maggie shook her head. "Just watching the snowstorm rolling in." And watching him. Jake was far more interesting than the snow.

He stood there with this attention fastened to the laptop, unaware that she was undressing him with her eyes. Maggie had never seen him naked, but her imagination was pretty good when it came to filling in the blanks.

The top two buttons of his shirt were undone, and she got a peek of the dark chest hair. Then, he turned, lifting his foot onto the metal ring on the bar stool that was several inches off the ground, and it gave her a good view of his butt and the Wranglers that were snug in all the right places.

Both front and back.

The only word that came to mind was *hot*. And the warning—Don't Play with Fire. She'd never melted looking at a man's zipper area, but she thought it might happen now.

Jake didn't take his hands off the keyboard, but he looked over at her as if he sensed something was going on. Great. Now she was looking head-on at that face. And his eyes. Those sizzling blue eyes were a storm of a different kind.

His stubble was past the fashionable stage, but it made him look like a cowboy outlaw. His black hair was rumpled. Bedroom hair.

If she went closer to him now, she could kiss him. Encourage him toward hauling her off to bed. She wanted that. Mercy, did she. But Maggie forced herself to think of the consequences, and one of the worst was that Jake might hate her and himself. She didn't want that. So, this had to be his decision. She couldn't set things into motion by asking for sex.

Even no-strings-attached sex.

Maggie waited for him to say something. Anything. But he just stared at her. Then, swallowed hard.

"How bad of a mistake would it be?" he asked, and there was no doubt what he meant.

"You tell me," she settled for saying. She saw the debate in his eyes. The heat, too. The heat was winning out, and she thought any second Jake would cross the room, pull her into his arms and, well, do whatever he wanted to do to her.

But instead he cursed, a very bad word, before he checked his watch. "I'm guessing you should get some rest. It'll be a long night."

It sounded like an order, or maybe he was just trying to convince himself. Either way, it wasn't an invitation, that was for sure. However, the heat was still there in his eyes, and his jaw muscles were way too tight for a man at peace with his decision.

"You're sure?" she asked, but she had to clear her throat and repeat it so it'd have some sound.

He said that bad word again and paired it with "No."

This time, Maggie saw something else paired with the heat. The frustration and even some torture. She certainly hadn't intended for Jake to feel that. She'd tortured him enough already.

"I'll get some rest," she concluded. Maggie didn't wait to see if he'd change his mind. That's because she was afraid she would change *hers*.

She walked to the guest room and didn't look back.

Chapter Fifteen

Hell.

He'd blown it.

Jake glanced at the bedroom door where Maggie had just disappeared. Then, he forced himself not to glance at it again just seconds later. He halfway expected her to come back out and force him to deal with this attraction between them.

She didn't.

The door stayed shut.

Too bad his brain and body didn't take it as a sign that he should keep it that way. He knew this was a mistake. In just a few hours, after the bone marrow procedure, Maggie would have to leave. He might never see her again. Knowing that, it was wrong to sleep with her.

That didn't stop him from wanting her.

Jake considered a shot of whiskey but didn't need anything else playing into this. His head was clear. And he had no excuses for what he was about to do.

He headed down the hall toward the spare bedroom where Maggie had gone. But he only made it a couple of steps before she opened the door and came out.

"I was listening for your footsteps." She frowned as if she hadn't wanted to admit that to him.

"I was waiting for you to open the door," he admitted right back.

The corner of her mouth lifted into a partial smile, but the amusement didn't make it to the rest of her expression. There was the fire. On her face. In the way she drew in a thin breath. And even the partial smile vanished when she stepped toward him at the same moment Jake stepped toward her.

They met, their mouths coming together at once.

It was as if they were starved for each other, and the kiss was hard, long and deep. Instant erection, but that didn't surprise him. He stayed pretty much aroused whenever he was around Maggie.

Jake cupped the back of her head, anchoring her in place against his mouth and his body, but Maggie did some anchoring of her own. She slung her arm around his waist and dragged him as close to her as he could get.

Well, he could get closer, if he was inside her.

He had no doubts that would happen soon but maybe not soon enough because he was already burning for her. Judging from Maggie's impatient, hungry hands, she felt the same. Her fingers dug into his back. Then lower. And she pressed him against her sex. The fit was right.

Without breaking the kiss, he moved Maggie toward the doorway, but Jake's shoulder rammed into the doorjamb. That only added to the stars he was already seeing, but it darn sure didn't slow them down. They turned, in some awkward dance that got them across the room and to the bed.

They tumbled onto the mattress. Maggie on top. With her leg pressed right against his erection. She reached her hands between them to unbutton his shirt. She pushed it open and then pulled away from him, her gaze going from his face to his now bare chest.

She made a sound. An erotic little hitch of breath that went through him and made him even harder, something he hadn't thought possible. With that sound still purring in his ears, she ran her hands over his chest. And lower. To his stomach.

Then lower.

Oh, man.

This was the best form of torture.

With her gaze locked with his, she undid his belt, shoved down his zipper and slid her hand to the only place he wanted it to slide.

Now, it was Jake's turn to make a sound. Not the breathy hitch that Maggie had made. His was more of a groan, throaty and deep. Not exactly a request for more, but she had the proof of what he wanted in her hand.

It didn't take long for her touch to fire up the need to finish this now, and Jake reached up and pulled off her sweater. Her bra was white, no lace or frills, and he unhooked it so her breasts spilled out into his hands. She was small, firm. Perfect. But touching wasn't enough. He dragged her closer so he could take her right nipple into his mouth.

Maggie made that sound again and melted back onto the mattress. It gave him good access to her pants, and while Jake kissed her breasts, then her stomach, he peeled off her jeans, taking her panties with them.

"Yeah, perfect," he said.

Her face, flushed with arousal. Her nipples, drawn and tight. She was breathing through her mouth now. And her lips were trembling. Fingers, too. But there was no fear on her face or in her eyes. The trembling was from need.

Jake upped that a little more.

He slid his hand down her stomach and between her legs so he could touch her. He wanted to see the pleasure on her face, while he was still capable of seeing. Once he was inside her, all chance of that was gone. So, he touched now. Slipping his fingers into her sex. Into all that wet heat.

He did more than tremble. Maggie jolted at his touch, and she grabbed on to handfuls of the bedding, bunching them into her fists. She made that sound again. Lifted her hips and let him touch her just the way he wanted.

"I'm toast," she mumbled.

Jake knew exactly how she felt.

He could feel her already close to a climax, but he didn't want her there yet. He wanted to be inside her when she came so he shifted their positions, adjusting.

And then he cursed.

Maggie's eyes widened, and she caught onto him when he started to move away. "You're not stopping."

"No condom," he said.

She cursed, too. "Surely, Royce has got one around here somewhere."

Oh, yeah. His brother was no saint and definitely not celibate.

Jake kissed her and slid his gaze down her naked, waiting body. "Hold that thought."

He got off her and hurried into the bathroom that divided the two bedrooms. Jake found not one but two boxes of condoms in the medicine cabinet. He'd thank his little brother later, but for now, he took one. Then, a second.

He hurried back to the bedroom and tossed one of the condoms on the nightstand. Maggie helped first with taking off his jeans and boxers and then helped with the condom. At least she tried, but her touch was like a lightning rod, and by the time they had the condom in place, Jake figured foreplay was over. Maggie clearly felt the same because she latched on to him and pulled him back on top of her.

Jake slid inside her. He tried to brace himself for the blinding pleasure, but this was a bracing kind of situation. Oh, mercy. He was toast, too.

"It's not supposed to feel this good," Maggie whispered.

Jake's thoughts were leaning in that same direction, and he blamed it on the fact that it'd likely been a while since either of them had done this.

He moved inside her. Slowly at first. But the need soon dictated the speed. She opened her body to him, wrapping her legs around his waist and lifting her hips with each trust. It didn't take long—not nearly long enough—before he felt the tremors of her climax.

She turned her head to the side, into the soft mattress, so that he couldn't see her face. Even with the blinding heat ramming through him, he wanted to see the pleasure there. He wanted to see what this was doing to her.

He kept up the thrusts inside her, but Jake took her by the chin, turning her and forcing the eye contact he needed.

And he saw it.

The moment that Maggie went over.

He felt it, in every part of his body. Every part of hers. The overwhelming need. Followed by the overwhelming release.

Her breath caught in her throat, and she pulled him closer. Closer. Closer. Until Jake could feel the release, the surrender. Completion.

He buried his face against the curve of Maggie's neck, and he let himself go.

He lay there, still buried deep inside her, and he let himself slowly come back to planet earth. Once he could catch a decent breath, Jake kissed her.

"I won't be long." And he headed into the bathroom for a moment.

He didn't look in the mirror. Didn't think. For just a

little while, he wanted to pretend that life felt as good as his satiated body. Maggie must have felt the same because, when he climbed in bed with her, she pulled him right into her arms and curved her body against his.

"When we screw things up," she whispered, "we do a thorough job of it."

"Yeah." But that didn't stop him from hauling her to him for another kiss. "Give me a half hour and we'll screw up things some more."

She chuckled, the motion rubbing her breasts against his chest, and just like that, he was ready again. Sheesh. He wasn't a teenager. He was thirty-five. But for the rest of their time together, Jake figured he would let this need, and Maggie, take over his common sense.

His phone buzzed, and Jake groaned. It was too soon to leave Maggie's arms and bed. Too soon to do much of anything, but then he remembered all the bad things that the good sex had made him temporarily forget.

Jake crawled his way to his jeans and rummaged through the pocket to come up with the phone. It was Royce's number he saw on the screen, and that nearly put him in a panic.

"Is something wrong with Sunny?" Jake asked the second he answered.

That question got Maggie moving, too. She wound the sheet around her and hurried to his side so she could listen.

"Sunny's fine and already tucked into bed for the night," Royce explained. "But we do have a problem. I got a call from Betsy Becker, and she saw someone suspicious in the parking lot at the Corral Junction hospital."

Neither Maggie nor Jake made a sound, but they both knew this couldn't be good. "Who was he?"

"We don't know yet. It a man in dark truck in the back

part of the parking lot. Betsy called the sheriff, and when he got out there, the guy sped away."

Yeah, definitely not good.

"I don't know how Tanner could have found out we were planning the procedure there. The only people who knew other than us were Becky and the doctor."

Jake scrubbed his hand over his face. "Maybe Tanner had someone planted in the hospital. He knows we need the bone marrow for Sunny."

And that meant Tanner might have hospitals staked out all around the area.

Hell.

"I could talk to the staff here," Royce suggested. "And see if they can do it."

"No." Jake didn't have to think about nixing that idea. "I don't want to give Tanner any reason to go after Sunny. Yeah, he probably did that bomb threat, but it was just that. A threat. And I think he was just playing games with Maggie and me. It's us he wants, and I don't want to lead him to Sunny or the rest of you."

Maggie whispered an agreement.

"So, what do we do?" Royce asked.

Nothing that would be totally safe, that was for sure. No matter which direction he went, it could be dangerous. The storm moving in certainly didn't help, either, because he didn't know how bad the roads would be. It wouldn't do Sunny any good if Maggie and he got into an accident.

Jake looked at Maggie to see if she had any say in this but she just stared back. "I trust you," she told him.

Great. Now she trusted him. He'd already planned to do whatever it took to keep her safe, but her trust upped the stakes. That and making love to her.

"Call Betsy," Jake said to Royce, "and see if she and

the doctor can meet Maggie and me at the Mustang Ridge hospital at midnight."

"Hell's bells, Jake. That's the last place you should go."

Maggie didn't curse, but she did give him a questioning stare.

"I'm hoping Mustang Ridge is the last place Tanner thinks we'll go," Jake explained. "And just in case he has someone already in place, I'll have Billy and Sheriff Marcus go through the entire hospital. Room by room. Once I have Maggie inside, the doors will be locked, and Billy and Marcus can secretly stand guard so that if Tanner's hired gun drives by, he won't be suspicious."

"You think that'll be enough?" Royce asked.

Jake hoped so. "Just protect Sunny," he said, and he ended the call.

"You still trust me?" he asked Maggie.

She nodded. "With my life."

It was the answer he wanted and dreaded at the same time. Because both hers and Sunny's lives were in his hands.

Chapter Sixteen

Maggie tried not to look afraid. That was hard to do. It wasn't the procedure that frightened her. No, the sooner they had the marrow, the sooner Sunny could get better. But what frightened her were all the things that could go wrong at the Mustang Ridge hospital.

Like an attack.

Jake was armed and ready, and they'd left Billy hidden away at the front entrance of the building. Sheriff Marcus was standing guard at the back. And since there were only four inpatients at the hospital, all on the second floor, there was minimal staff. Added to that, they were doing the marrow harvesting in a surgical room in the part of the hospital that was completely deserted, and it would stay that way unless there was some kind of emergency that required the use of the room. Even then, Jake had assured her they'd have notice so she could be moved if necessary.

But not notice through his cell phone.

There was no service in this part of the hospital since it was also where radiology was located. However, both Billy and the sheriff had been given the landline number.

"Everything will be fine," Betsy whispered to Maggie, though she heard the concern in the nurse's voice. She saw it in the doctor's eyes, too, when he walked closer to the surgical gurney and looked down at her.

Dr. Allen Blake. The tall, lanky doctor looked barely old enough to be out of medical school, but Betsy had assured Maggie that he knew what he was doing. "I have to ask again if there's any part of this you want to reconsider." He had some forms attached to a clipboard, but he didn't offer them to her.

"No," Maggie insisted. "I'm going through with this." She glanced at Jake, who was wearing a surgical mask and standing guard by the door.

That didn't seem to please the doctor. Probably because he'd already tried to talk her into having a general anesthesia. Maggie had declined, opting for a local instead. She didn't want to be asleep in case something went wrong, even though the doctor had warned her that she'd be more *comfortable* with the general because the local would only numb the area when he'd need to inject the harvesting needle.

Maybe that *comfortable* would apply to physical pain but not to anything else.

Dr. Blake had finally conceded to her wishes and had given her a shot in her right pelvic bone. She was already numb and anxious to get on with this.

She took the clipboard from Dr. Blake and signed the release form. "Let's do this now," she insisted.

Thank goodness he didn't continue to argue. He disappeared for several minutes and came back scrubbed and ready to go.

"If we had more time," the doctor explained, talking through his surgical mask, "I could give you a drug to stimulate growth of your stem cells, and we could extract them through your blood."

"But you said it would take five days," Maggie pointed out. "I want my niece to get the marrow tonight."

Maggie shut out his response. She shut out everything

when she felt the pressure from needle into her pelvic bone. Then, the pain.

Oh, yes.

There was pain.

She tried not to grimace or react, but she made the mistake of glancing at Jake. He knew her too well and saw right through the facade, and even though she couldn't hear what he said, she thought he was mumbling, "I'm sorry."

Hopefully, the pain was the only thing he was sorry for.

They hadn't had a chance to discuss the fact they'd had sex, and even though that might be a troubling conversation, Maggie concentrated on it now. It was far better than thinking about the pain.

Soon, if he hadn't already, she figured Jake would go through a major guilt trip. Sleeping with her probably felt like a betrayal to Anna, his marriage and the family they'd created together.

Maggie felt some of that, as well.

She loved her sister and missed her, but Maggie's feelings for Jake ran deep. There was no way she could turn that off, especially after the mind-blowing sex. She'd been right about them screwing up things in a big way. She didn't regret what they'd done, but she would have to come to terms with the consequences.

Jake, too.

Maybe he would see this as a new beginning of sorts. Not necessarily with Maggie. But the start to the next phase of his life. Anna certainly wouldn't have expected Jake to live like a monk.

Maggie glanced at Jake again and saw that he was volleying looks between the hall, the needle and her. His forehead was bunched up. His eyes were strained.

I'm okay, she mouthed to him. And she just kept repeating it to herself.

Maggie didn't know how much time passed, and she didn't look at the clock. Or the doctor. Especially not at the needle. She focused only on Sunny's face and let the minutes crawl by.

"We're done," she finally heard the doctor say, and it seemed as if all three of them had a collective sigh of relief. "I have a medical courier on standby. I hadn't told him my location for security reasons, but I'll obviously have to tell him now. I'll get him over here so he can transport this to the hospital in Amarillo."

Yet one more obstacle, but hopefully this would be easy.

"Make sure the courier has the two guards with him that I hired," Jake added.

Maggie had known about the guards because Jake had called to arrange them while they were still at Royce's house. She welcomed the extra security. After everything they'd been through, nothing was overkill.

The doctor left the room with the harvested marrow, and Betsy bandaged the area around the injection site. "You'll be numb for at least another half hour," Betsy explained. The nurse turned to Jake. "Wait here with her while I get her some pain meds. She'll need them once the local anesthesia wears off."

Jake nodded, and while he continued to keep watch from the doorway, he took off his mask. Betsy went through the other door where the doctor had gone earlier.

"I don't know how I can ever thank you for this," Jake said.

Maggie didn't want his thanks. And got a little queasy when she realized what she wanted was Jake.

Oh, yes. Now, she was headed to fantasyland. Because a life with Jake was the one thing she couldn't have. He'd already told her that when they left the hospital, he'd drive her to the marshals' office in Amarillo where she'd no doubt be reprocessed for WITSEC. Soon, the McCalls might have to do the same unless they wanted to live the rest of their lives looking over their shoulders for Tanner.

"No need to thank me," Maggie finally answered. "I just want what you want—for Sunny to be okay. And if this doesn't work, if she needs more marrow harvested, I'll make sure you have a way to get in touch with me. No more do-not-contact orders."

He nodded. Glanced into the hall again and then came across the room. Jake dropped a gentle kiss on her lips, looked deeply into her eyes and brushed his hand across her hair before he walked back to the door to stand guard.

It was hardly the hot embrace they'd had at Royce's, but it somehow seemed more intimate.

Maggie turned toward the other doorway when she heard the phone ring in the other room. Then, the hurried footsteps, and a moment later, Betsy appeared. One look at her face, and Maggie knew something was wrong.

"Billy just called," Betsy said. She had a death grip on the phone in her hand. "Someone's here."

JAKE'S HEART SLAMMED against his chest.

In thirty minutes, maybe less, he could have gotten Maggie out of there. She would have been on her way to safety.

Judging from Maggie's stark expression, she felt the same. She didn't have much color in her cheeks, but that pretty much drained what was there. She shook her head, whispered something. Maybe a prayer. They might need a boatload of them before the night was over.

Jake motioned for Betsy to bring him the phone, and the woman rushed across the room to hand it to him. "What's wrong? Who's here?" he immediately asked Billy.

"A black van just drove up and parked about twenty

feet from the door. Could be nothing, but I got an uneasy feeling about it."

So did Jake, and he hadn't even seen the van. Of course, anybody's arrival at this point would put him on edge. Unless…

Jake snagged Betsy's attention. "Ask the doctor if the medical courier would arrive in a black van."

Betsy shook her head. "I already asked, the second Billy told me. The courier's still fifteen minutes out, but he does have the two guards with him that you hired."

Jake didn't want the courier walking into this, but he wouldn't mind having the guards as backup. But fifteen minutes wouldn't be nearly fast enough. If Tanner's men were out there in the parking lot.

He was betting they were.

"Keep me posted," he said to Billy, and Jake pressed the end-call button. He turned to Betsy again. "Where's the doctor right now?"

"In the lab. He's processing the marrow. It has to be tested before the courier picks it up."

Jake didn't want to delay the testing, especially if it could delay Sunny getting the donation, but he couldn't risk the doctor or Betsy's lives. "Is there a lock on the lab door?"

She nodded.

"Go there, lock the door and stay put. Call me on this landline if anything goes wrong."

Betsy turned to hurry away, but Jake thought of something else. Something he didn't want to consider, but he had no choice. "If things get bad here, call the courier and tell him to stay away from the hospital until I can get things under control."

Another shaky nod, and Betsy practically ran out of the surgical suite.

Maggie moved, too. Using her elbows, she tried to lever herself up. "If Tanner's men get inside in the building, the surgical suites are the first places they'll look for us."

Jake didn't doubt that. He had to get Maggie out of there, just in case, and he needed to do it now.

"Wait," he insisted when she tried to get up again. There was no way she could walk just yet.

Jake went to her and handed her the phone so it would free up his left hand. He kept his gun gripped in his right, and despite the adrenaline punch, he forced himself to stay gentle. His instincts were to grab her and run, but he didn't want to hurt her after all the pain she'd just gone through.

"Where are we going?" she asked.

"To the back, where Sheriff Marcus is. We might be able to get out that way." He returned to the door and peered out into the hall.

No one was there, thank God.

With Maggie in his arms, Jake left the suite and went right—toward the back of the hospital, in the opposite direction of the black van.

There was a set of stairs there, an elevator, too, but Jake didn't want to go to the second floor since that's where the patients were. If there was trouble, he didn't want to endanger sick or hurt people who were incapable of defending themselves.

Maggie fell into that category.

Jake couldn't allow her to be hurt. Not after everything she'd done for Sunny and him. He had to get her safely out of there.

The Mustang Ridge hospital wasn't big by any means, and it didn't take Jake long to work his way from the surgical area, through a set of double doors and to the back exit.

"It's me," Jake called out when he made it to the hall where Sheriff Marcus was standing guard.

The sheriff already had his gun drawn, and his attention was fastened to the back parking lot. "Billy called me," Marcus said, glancing back at them. "And I was just about to call you. An SUV just drove up and parked."

Jake cursed. It was too early for the courier, which meant Tanner had likely planned for both exits to be covered. No escape route. It was a smart move for Tanner. A bad one for them.

Marcus tipped his head to Maggie. "You should probably get her away from this door."

Jake agreed, especially since Maggie was making small, muffled sounds of discomfort. But he didn't want to go too far from the exit in case Marcus needed backup. He hurried up the hall and tested the knobs on the closed doors. The first two were locked so he rounded the corner at the end of the hall and started trying the doors there.

Finally, he found one unlocked. It was the waiting area of a pediatric office.

He didn't turn on the overhead lights, but there was enough illumination coming from the hall that Jake could see that the room was filled with chairs and small tables piled high with books and toys. There was a reception desk, closed off with a partition and a glass window. That part was locked, too, and so was the adjacent door that led into the doctor's office.

Of course, it was possible that someone could unlock that office door from inside since it likely had an exterior entrance in the T-shaped building. Plus, there was the window. Not exactly his first choice for security. He was in the middle of a quick debate about what to do when Maggie made another of those muffled sounds.

Jake looked down at her and saw the pain on her face. "I'm okay," she insisted.

No, hell, no, she wasn't. The numbness was wearing

off, and here he was jiggling her all around. That ended his debate, and he took her to the corner by the partition— away from the window. It was close to the locked office door but at least out of the line of sight of the hall. Jake eased her onto the floor. Not ideal, but if Tanner was indeed about to launch an attack, there was nothing ideal about their situation.

Jake checked his phone and saw that he actually had service in this part of the building. That was something at least. Now Billy, the doctor and Betsy had two ways to contact him. His family, too, but he prayed that wouldn't be necessary. He hoped that Sunny was asleep and dreaming of the Christmas presents she'd get to open soon.

"Give me your backup weapon," Maggie insisted.

He actually had two backup weapons, and he took the small Smith & Wesson from his boot holster. "This might turn out to be nothing." He hoped.

She nodded and, while her eyes said she was hoping the same thing, Maggie took the gun and maneuvered herself into a sitting position. She took aim at the door.

A shaky aim.

"I'll try to get you out of here as soon as possible," he promised. He especially wanted to do that before the rest of the numbness wore off.

Maggie's gaze met his. "Kiss me," she whispered.

He stared at her, cursed. "I'm not kissing you goodbye."

She huffed. "Not goodbye. Just kiss me. And then get your butt to the door and keep watch."

In a potentially dangerous situation, Jake normally wouldn't have taken the time for a kiss. But this was Maggie, and he wanted to kiss her. To reassure her. Heck, to reassure himself.

Jake leaned in, and he touched his mouth to hers. Just a gentle brush of their lips before he increased the pressure. Before he slid his hand around the back of her neck so he could angle her head and kiss her the way he really wanted. It was longer, harder and deeper than he'd planned, but Jake was glad that it was one plan that had gone south.

He'd needed that kiss as much as Maggie apparently had.

Their gazes connected again when he eased back. Just a few seconds, and Jake knew that was all they were going to get. For now anyway. Maybe this would be over soon, and he could get her out of there.

The thought had no sooner crossed his mind when there was a slight crackling sound, and the lights went out. The office was instantly plunged into darkness.

"Marcus?" Jake called out. He hurried to the door and glanced out into the hall, but it was too dark for him to see the sheriff.

"I didn't turn them off," Marcus answered.

Another jolt of adrenaline slammed through Jake because he doubted this was a coincidence. Yeah, it was snowing, but it wasn't nearly bad enough to knock out the power.

He waited, listening, but the only sounds he could hear were Maggie's and his breaths and his own heartbeat in his ears. The seconds ticked off in his head, but he didn't hear something he should have heard.

The generator kicking in.

Jake knew the hospital had one, and it should have turned on by now.

"Tanner's men did this," Maggie mumbled.

Yeah, they'd likely tampered with it, and it made him wonder what else they'd tampered with.

"Call Betsy," he told Maggie. "I don't want her moving from wherever she is, but I need her to phone someone on the second floor. It needs to be shut down. I don't want any of Tanner's men able to access it."

Or the patients there.

He kept watch at the door while Maggie did that, and Jake hoped it would be enough. There weren't any other emergency personnel he could request for backup tonight except for the fire department, which would already be on call. But he didn't want them walking into a dangerous situation since they wouldn't even be armed.

"Jake?" Marcus called out. "We got a problem."

"What?" he asked, and prayed it that it would be a problem with a quick, safe answer.

"Get down!" Marcus shouted a split second later.

And the sound of a gunshot blasted through the building.

Chapter Seventeen

Maggie's heart jumped to her throat. *No.* This couldn't be happening. That shot couldn't have hit Sheriff Marcus, not after he'd tried to so hard to help them.

She listened for any sound, anything to indicate if the sheriff was dead or alive, and Maggie tried to aim the gun Jake had given her.

No easy feat.

Her hands were wobbly. Her entire body was. Except for the part of her where the doctor had drawn the bone marrow. The numbness was wearing off fast, and the pain was starting to throb. Maggie tried to push the pain aside and concentrate on the sheriff, Jake and staying alive.

"They're not in the building," Marcus finally shouted. "Not yet anyway."

The relief caused her breath to stall in her lungs. Marcus hadn't been shot. He was alive and at least well enough to talk. She prayed he stayed that way.

"How many are out there?" Jake asked.

"Can't tell. They fired the shot from an open window of the vehicle, and it came through the back door. I'm not sure what the bullet hit."

The door was made of reinforced glass, the kind with metal webbing in the center. It wouldn't stop a bullet or prevent a break-in, but it would hopefully slow the men down.

The phone in Maggie's lap rang, and she quickly answered it so that the ringing sound wouldn't help their attackers pinpoint their position.

"It's me, Billy," the man said, through rough gusts of breath. "They just got out of the van. Two of them. Dressed in camo, and they're heavily armed."

Oh, God. She relayed the news to Jake, but as soon as she finished, she heard Billy's voice again.

"They're coming straight for the front door." His words came out so fast that they ran together. "It's locked, but they could shoot their way in."

And no doubt would.

"Get away from the door, Billy," Maggie ordered. "Don't try to fight these guys head-on, but if you get a chance, take them out."

She glanced at Jake and saw the fear and concern in the glimpse that he gave her. It was a risk to have bullets flying with patients on the second floor. Maybe the ceilings were reinforced so a shot couldn't get through. But there'd be an even greater risk to the patients, and them, if the gunmen took control of the place. They might have orders to eliminate all potential witnesses.

"Watch the elevators," Maggie warned Billy. "They can't get to the second floor."

"I understand."

And when Billy hung up, she turned off the phone's ringer. If he called back, Maggie would still see the caller-ID screen light up, but she couldn't risk the gunmen following the sound of a ring.

The front part of the building was too far away for Maggie to hear what was going on there, but maybe Billy would have a chance to keep them updated. She hoped that Billy would be able to defuse whatever was going on at the front of the building.

"The SUV door just opened," Sheriff Marcus relayed to them. "Two men. Maybe more. I think there's someone else in the backseat. But the two I see are wearing ski masks, and they're armed to the hilt."

That didn't help steady her already raw nerves. With the two at the front of the building, they had at least four gunmen converging on the building. Yes, there were four of them with Billy and the sheriff, but Maggie figured she was nowhere up to holding off an attack.

Still, that wouldn't stop her.

She could barely move her body, but she had a gun and she could shoot.

Maggie thought of Dr. Blake and Betsy and hoped they'd managed to find a place to hide. The best way to keep them and that marrow safe was to make sure the gunmen didn't get deep into the building so they could attack anyone. That was no doubt exactly what Jake was thinking, too.

There was another shot, and she could tell from the sound of it that it had been fired closer to them than the first. The gunmen were definitely on the move.

The next shot proved that.

It slammed first through the window and then inside. Without the reinforced glass to hold them back, that'd make it much easier for the gunmen to get in the building.

"Get back!" Jake yelled to the sheriff.

But Jake didn't take his own advice.

He leaned out into the hall and fired.

Maggie wanted to shout for Jake to at least take better cover behind the doorjamb, but he stayed put, with his gun ready and aimed.

More shots came from the back of the building, and in between those rounds, Maggie heard the sound of the door being bashed in.

Followed by footsteps.

Jake pivoted, leaning out so he could fire a shot. It blasted through the air. And it wasn't the only blast. Two bullets came Jake's way, blistering past him as he ducked back inside the room.

He cursed. "Sheriff Marcus is down," he said.

And Jake leaned out from cover and started firing.

THE BULLETS CAME AT HIM, but Jake didn't stop shooting. He couldn't. He had to give Sheriff Marcus a fighting chance to stay alive.

Using the sides of the exterior building for cover, the two gunmen bashed their weapons against what was left of the door, and it didn't take them long to finish the job. Jake could barely see them in the shadows, but they came through firing nonstop.

One of them, the guy on the right, focused on Jake, the other on Marcus, who had already been shot in the shoulder. Jake knew that because he'd seen the bullet slam into the man.

Marcus dove to the side, into the room at that end of the building, and Jake heard the sound of the door slamming. Hopefully, Marcus had a way to lock it so he could regroup. Maybe, just maybe, his injury wasn't so bad that he wouldn't bleed out before he could get medical attention.

God knew when that would be.

He doubted any of the medical staff could or would respond with all the bullets flying. Jake hoped that was true anyway. He didn't need anyone else shot tonight.

One the men tried to open the door where Marcus had disappeared. The other made a beeline for Jake.

Jake fired at him, and the guy ducked behind a medical cart loaded with equipment. He shot at the other guy, too, and sent him scurrying to the recessed area to the left. Good. At least he had them pinned down. For the moment anyway.

The moment didn't last long.

The man behind the cart took aim at Jake and fired. He had to jump back so he wouldn't be shot, and the bullet tore away a chunk of the doorjamb where he'd just been standing.

Maggie cursed. "Are you trying to get yourself killed? Stay back."

Jake hated the fear in her voice. The worry. It was for him, but his worry was for her. If he didn't end this now, Tanner's men would somehow get to Maggie.

Another shot slammed into the jamb. Then another.

Jake had lost count of how many times the gunman had fired, but he figured he'd have to reload soon. Jake did something to help that along. He grabbed some of the hard plastic building blocks from one of the tables and he tossed them out into the hall.

The guy fired again.

And again.

Jake stuck out his hand and fired, too. That left him seven more shots, and he had two magazines of extra ammo in his pockets. Of course, he didn't want to take the time to reload, either. Especially with two gunmen this close and more God knew where in the hospital. He wanted to do some damage control now.

He threw out another handful of blocks.

The shots came.

And Jake timed it so that at the first pause, he leaned out, took aim and fired. Since he couldn't risk just wounding this assassin, he double tapped the trigger, and both shots went into the guy's chest. He flew back, slamming into the wall and gasping.

Jake fired another shot. This time to the head, just in case the guy was wearing Kevlar.

One down.

Three to go.

And the most immediate threat was the guy in the recessed area. He started shooting, and the man had far better cover that his fallen comrade since he was concealed behind thick block wall. At least he couldn't head upstairs and loop around behind them since there was no way out of there. Of course, maybe he didn't want to escape. He was probably loaded down with extra ammo and could shoot up the entire place.

He was certainly doing a good job of tearing apart the doorjamb that Jake was using for cover.

Jake heard other shots, too. Not nearby. But from the other side of the building where Billy was. The two gunmen had no doubt gotten into the building, and Billy was alone without backup. Jake wished there was a way to get to him, to help, but he wouldn't make it an inch in the hall without getting shot. Plus, he couldn't leave Maggie alone for even a second.

The guy in the recessed area kept shooting, but the others stopped. Jake prayed that was a good sign, but he knew full well it could go the other way.

Behind him, Jake saw a flash of light, and when Maggie put the phone to her ear, he realized someone had called.

"Billy," she relayed in a whisper.

Hell. He hoped his deputy was okay. Billy was a good lawman, but he was young and had never faced anything like this.

"He took out one of them," Maggie said. "But the other got away. Billy thinks he's on his way back here."

Jake felt the punch of relief that his deputy was alive, but there wasn't much relief in another killer headed their way.

"Tell Billy to protect the doctor, Betsy and the others," Jake said.

Yeah, it was a risk. Jake might need the deputy to help with the gunman, but it could be an even bigger risk for Billy to try to get to the rear of the hospital where they were.

Maggie repeated to Billy what Jake had told her, and she paused. A moment later, she clicked the button to end the call.

"Billy said the gunman headed our way is using some kind of handheld device to pinpoint us," she added in a whisper. "Maybe a thermal scan."

Jake would have cursed if a hail of bullets hadn't come right at them. More of the doorjamb went, and the bullets tore through a part of the wall.

Bullet by bullet, the gunman was taking away Jake's cover, and if he managed to do that, Jake would have no choice but to move back where he wouldn't be able to fire until the gunman was right on them. Jake glanced back at Maggie and the locked office door near her. "Try to open it," he said. Because it might be the fastest way to shield her from the gunmen.

Jake heard the movement at the rear door. Heard the footsteps, too.

And he cursed.

It wasn't Sheriff Marcus, that was for sure, because Jake hadn't heard the man open the door where he'd taken shelter. Marcus had likely been right about someone else being in the backseat because this person was coming from the outside and into the building.

Another gunman, no doubt.

It made Jake wonder just how many assassins Tanner had sent after them. And how many more he'd continue to send. Yeah, if they got out of this alive, he'd have to move Maggie and the others far out of Tanner's reach.

If that was possible.

"Don't shoot," the man said.

Jake froze because he recognized that voice.

"It's David," Maggie whispered, obviously recognizing the voice, too.

Well, now they knew the identity of Tanner's latest accomplice. His own son.

Not a surprise.

But it did surprise Jake that David had asked him not to shoot. Jake had no plans to negotiate with David or any of Tanner's goons.

"Don't shoot," David repeated. His voice was broken. A terrified tremble.

Jake figured that particular emotion could be faked, but it sure didn't sound it.

"If you shoot me," David said, "you'll kill us all."

Well, that got his attention and didn't let go.

"It could be a trap," Maggie reminded him.

Yeah. Jake was anticipating that. He didn't trust David any more than he did Tanner. But what puzzled Jake was why the shots had stopped.

Jake scurried to the other side of the door so he could get a better look while still keeping a small amount of cover. He glanced out and nearly froze from the stunned surprise.

In that glimpse, he saw David, his hands lifted high into the air as if surrendering.

"Please don't shoot," David begged.

Jake risked another glance out into the hall.

Oh, hell.

Things had just gone from bad to worse.

Chapter Eighteen

Maggie could tell from the sound that Jake made that this wasn't good news.

She'd heard David, of course, heard his pleadings for Jake not to shoot, but obviously Jake saw something that made him hold fire. It had to be something critical, a game changer, because there's no way Jake would have trusted Bruce Tanner's son.

David was their most obvious suspect.

Since Jake's attention was fastened to whatever was going on out there in the hall, Maggie turned and tried to unlock the door.

"David's got what appears to be a bomb strapped to his chest," Jake said. "It looks real."

"It *is* real," David shouted. "That SOB you just killed popped me with a stun gun earlier when I was going to my car, and he put this thing on me."

Oh, God.

Maggie had figured it was something bad, but she hadn't counted on it being this *bad*. Bullets were one thing, but a bomb could do a lot of damage, including kill everyone in the building.

The bone marrow might even be destroyed.

It broke her heart to think that Sunny might not get what she needed to live. And if she was killed in an explosion,

Sunny would have no other donor. It was as if Tanner was giving Sunny a death sentence, too.

That infuriated her.

And terrified her.

She worked even harder to get the office door open. It might not help to get to another room, especially if there were a lot of explosives strapped to David, but she wanted to get Jake and her as far away from that bomb as possible. Sheriff Marcus, too, though she wasn't sure he could hear her if she shouted for him to take cover. Maybe, though, he could hear David and Jake and had already done whatever he could to protect himself.

"Does the bomb have a timer on it?" Maggie asked, though she wasn't sure she wanted to know the answer. In her mind, she could see the seconds ticking away to their deaths.

"Not that I can see," Jake answered. "But it appears to be sticks of dynamite taped to some kind of vest."

"The sticks are all wired together, I don't know who has the detonator," David added. "But the dead guy said it would go off on impact."

In other words, if Jake shot David, the whole place might blow up. It was a good thing Jake hadn't shot David on sight. They might already be dead.

That got her working even harder.

The pain was running through her hip and side, but Maggie used the doorknob and wall to lever herself higher. Every inch was an effort, and she was in a cold sweat by the time she made it to her knees.

"Do the hired guns know Tanner sent them on a suicide mission?" Jake asked. Not for David's sake. But probably to rattle the gunmen.

She knew Jake had killed one of the men. She'd heard the bullets as they'd thudded into him. And according to

Billy, one of the men on his end of the building was dead, too, but that left two others.

And David.

This bomb thing could be a hoax designed to draw them out into the open. In fact, it was exactly the kind of stunt Tanner would pull.

"No, I don't think they know," David growled. "They're no doubt in this for the money. Well, money's not going to do you any good if you're blown to smithereens."

If the gunmen had any reaction whatsoever to that, Maggie didn't hear it. Maybe, though, Jake could keep working on them, though she figured even if the bomb wasn't a hoax, it might take a miracle to get the gunmen to surrender.

"I need to shoot the lock on the door," she told Jake when she couldn't get it to budge.

He volleyed glances between her and the hall, and even though it was too dark to see his face clearly, Maggie knew the debate that was going on there. He didn't want her moving around. Especially since she was gasping every time the muscles moved in her hip.

That seemed to be with every movement.

But he couldn't very well leave David and the other gunmen unguarded to help her with a door.

"Shield your eyes," Jake reminded her.

She did. Maggie took aim at the lock, turned her head to the side and fired.

The sound was deafening, the metal bullet ripping through the metal lock, and the jolt seemed to go through her entire body, rattling and shaking her. Not good. Because it also rattled the pain, and it hit her so hard that she had to fight to keep hold of her breath.

While she kept a grip on the gun with her right hand, Maggie used her shoulder to push the door open. Finally.

She hadn't counted on it opening so easily, though, and with her thigh still partly numb, she wasn't able to stop her forward momentum in time.

She tumbled through the opening and braced herself to smack face-first onto the floor.

But she didn't.

That's because someone in the pitch black reached out for her. Caught her, too. But it wasn't to save her, Maggie soon realized.

No.

The person knocked her weapon from her hand, dragged her to her feet.

And he put a gun to her head.

JAKE HEARD MAGGIE'S GASP, and he reeled in that direction only to see her being dragged into the other room.

"Maggie?" he shouted.

No answer.

The fear crawled through him, and he kicked the hall door shut. Locked it, too, even though the door frame was so damaged he didn't know if the lock would hold. It didn't matter.

Nothing mattered at this point but Maggie.

He braced his right wrist with his left hand and moved toward the room. The doctor's office. And he prayed he'd find her alive.

He made a quick peek into the room and saw the partially open exterior door that led straight into the office. And he saw Maggie. She was there, standing, among all the shadows. Except she wasn't exactly standing on her own. Someone was behind her, and the person had an arm curved around her waist. Anchoring her in place.

"Stay back," Maggie warned him. "He'll shoot you."

Jake was staying back, using the wall and jamb for

cover, but he couldn't stop himself from taking another quick look.

"I'm sorry," she whispered. "I didn't see him until it was too late."

Jake hated that she felt the need to apologize for being taken hostage. And there was no doubt that she was someone's hostage. The gun to her head was proof of that. But her captor was keeping his own head hidden behind hers.

"Who are you?" Jake asked.

"Why don't you come in here and find out?" the man said.

It was Wade.

And the slimeball actually sounded pleased with himself. Jake wished he could get close enough to tear the man limb from limb.

"Maggie shouldn't be standing," Jake said, though he knew it wouldn't do any good. He just wanted the idiot to poke out his head so Jake could get off a shot. "She's hurt."

"Hurt?" Wade grumbled. "You mean she had the harvesting done. Yeah, I know all about that. I'm supposed to collect that, too, in case Tanner needs it for some kind of leverage."

Tanner. Who else?

Since Jake still didn't have a clean shot, he tried again to get Wade to move. "I'm guessing the bomb's a fake or else you wouldn't be this close to it."

"It's real. Not enough explosives to kill us, but it would do David in. His dad is really pissed off at him. Wants him dead."

Hell. That was one bargaining angle that Jake couldn't use. He'd hoped that Wade didn't know about the bomb and would start running.

"Maybe there are more explosives on David than Tanner wanted you to know about," Jake tried.

"He wouldn't do that." And it didn't sound as if Wade had any doubts about his boss.

"How did you find us?" Maggie asked Wade. "How did you know we'd be here?"

Jake didn't miss the quick breath she sucked in at the end of her question. She was in pain. And in danger. It was killing him to stand there and do nothing while she suffered. But he couldn't just take any shot.

"Tanner had teams ready to go to various hospitals. He figured Mustang Ridge was the last place so that's why he put me with this group. I'm hardly a killer, you know."

"Yes, I know." And that was Jake's opening to keep pushing. "That's why you should let Maggie go."

"Not a chance. Once one of the other guys gets in here, he'll do the killings. And I'll get paid."

"The other guys?" Jake questioned. "Not Grange?"

Wade huffed. "Grange isn't in on this. Tanner could never trust a man like him."

"You mean Grange isn't greedy like you are."

"Yeah, so what? You were more than willing to pay me to hack into that database. Well, Tanner's paying me a whole lot more to do this."

So, if the other guy wasn't Grange, Wade was waiting on one of the two gunmen. Or maybe there were more.

Hell.

Tanner could have sent an entire army. But Jake held out hope that wasn't true. After all, Wade had just admitted that Tanner hadn't sent his best crew here because he hadn't expected Maggie and him to use the hospital in Mustang Ridge.

"You really think Tanner's going to let you live?" Maggie asked the man. "You're a loose end, Wade. A bad one."

"He's already on death row. Can't kill a man twice."

"Yeah, but Tanner has a reason to eliminate you," Jake

said. "If you confess to his hiring assassins, then the FBI can freeze his assets. All of them. Without money, Tanner has no power. So, it's my guess he'll arrange for you to have an accident."

Wade didn't come back with a smart-mouthed response so maybe he was thinking about it. Jake glanced in at Maggie again, but this time, Wade turned the gun toward him.

And he fired.

Jake jumped back in the nick of time, and even over the roar in his ears from the blast, he could still hear Maggie struggling.

No!

She wasn't in any shape to defend herself.

Jake turned, ready to look into the room to see what was happening, but before he could do that, he heard another sound. One from a different direction. That was the only warning he got before someone kicked down the hall door.

It came flying right at Jake.

Jake ducked and came up ready to fire. He did a split-second assessment to make sure it wasn't Billy or Marcus. It wasn't. It was one of Tanner's assassins dressed in camouflage. The guy had his gun already aimed at Jake.

But Jake fired first and dropped to the floor.

He fired again.

And the guy dropped, too. Dead.

Jake scrambled back to the doorway of the other room and saw the struggle going on. Maggie was against the desk, and she had Wade's right hand in a firm grip to stop him from firing. However, Wade was using his left hand to punch and hit Maggie on her face and chest.

Jake didn't even think.

He ran into the room, and he, too, latched on to Wade's wrist while he pushed Maggie out of the way. She fell into the wall, and it no doubt hurt, but at least she wasn't directly in front of Wade's gun.

The man pulled the trigger again, the shot blasting into the floor. And Jake knew enough was enough. He bashed his gun against Wade's head. Again and again. Until he finally dropped his weapon. It clattered onto the floor next to Maggie, and she scooped it up. She also grabbed her own gun that Wade had obviously knocked from her hands.

Jake didn't waste any time. He put his own gun directly to Wade's head. "Move and you die."

And Jake gave Wade a look to let him know that it wasn't a bluff.

Wade cursed, but he quit fighting. In fact, he practically went limp. It wasn't enough for Jake. He shoved the man to floor, putting him on his belly and facedown.

"Put your hands on the back of your head," Jake ordered.

Once Wade had done that, Jake looked at Maggie, afraid of what he might see. There was blood trickling down her mouth, and she was still unsteady because she had to catch on to the wall to keep from falling.

Jake went to her, just to try to reassure her and himself that she was indeed okay. She was. But they weren't out of this yet.

"I need something to tie up Wade," he told her after he ran his hand down her arm.

"Maybe use that." She tipped her head to the doctor's jacket that was on a hook on the wall.

It wasn't handcuffs, but maybe he could make it work. Jake snatched the jacket and went back toward Wade.

But he only made it one step before the sound of another shot stopped him cold.

MAGGIE'S MOUTH WENT DRY, and her breath stalled in her throat.

She waited to feel the shot slam through her. Or worse, to see it slam through Jake. But it took her a moment to realize neither had been hit. Not Wade, either.

The shot had come from the hall.

She allowed herself a moment of relief, but Maggie knew this wasn't good. Both Billy and Sheriff Marcus were somewhere out there. Dr. Allen Blake and Betsy, too. Plus, the patients and other staff. David was out there as well, and according to Wade he had a real bomb strapped to him.

Since Jake had his gun aimed at Wade, Maggie glanced into the room where Jake and she had been earlier, and she saw David run into the room. Even though this room was dark, too, it did have slightly more light because of the window.

And she got her first look at the bomb.

Maggie tried to back away from it. From David. But she could barely move.

"He's trying to kill me," David yelled. "And if he hits the bomb with one of those shots, we all die."

Maggie heard everything he said, but her attention wasn't on David but rather the gun he had in his hand. Even in the dim light, she had no trouble spotting it. He didn't have it aimed at her but rather at the doorway to the hall.

"You need to drop that weapon," Maggie told him, and she put Wade's gun on the desk she could aim her own weapon at David.

And at the hall.

Just in case the other killer made his move. Too bad she wasn't exactly a show of force since she had to latch on to the wall to keep from falling.

"What the hell is he doing?" Jake snarled, and with his gun still pointed at Wade, he rushed to the door.

The moment Jake's attention landed on David's gun, he stepped in front of her. "Keep an eye on Wade," Jake instructed, and he turned his attention to David.

Jake turned his gun on him, too, the moment that Maggie took aim at Wade, but as she'd done, Jake also kept his eye on the hall door.

"It's not my gun," David volunteered, glancing back at Jake. "I picked it up off the floor."

It'd belonged to the dead assassin no doubt, and while David still didn't seem to be threatening Jake and her with the weapon, she didn't want it in his hands.

Apparently, neither did Jake.

"This is your last warning," Jake told him. "Drop the gun. I can shoot you without hitting that bomb."

David looked behind him at Jake, and he no doubt saw that Jake wasn't bluffing. He'd shoot.

"Okay," David said, and he lowered himself toward the floor.

From over Jake's shoulder, Maggie saw the blur of motion in the hall door. Jake turned his gun from David toward the movement.

Toward the assassin who had a gun pointed right at them.

The shot echoed through the room, and in the murky darkness it took Maggie a moment to realize that Jake hadn't fired the shot.

David had.

The assassin froze and he dropped to the floor. David dropped the gun, too, and he went to the man and touched his fingers to his neck.

"Dead," David announced. "Is that the last of them?"

"I think so," Jake answered, but he didn't lower his gun. He kept it trained on David.

Maggie did the same to Wade. The man was still on

the floor, his hands on the back of his head, and he was cursing a blue streak.

With his left hand, Jake took out his phone and made a call, just a few words to give someone their location and request the bomb squad.

"Billy's on the way," he relayed to her. "And he'll check on Sheriff Marcus, too."

Good. That was a start, but Maggie wouldn't breathe easier until she was away from both Wade and David.

"I want a plea bargain, Sheriff McCall," Wade insisted, adding some more profanity. "I'll tell you everything you want to freeze Tanner's accounts, but you have to give me a written agreement that I won't get any jail time."

It sickened Maggie to think of slime like Wade going scot-free, but it sickened her more to think of Tanner being able to continue these attacks.

"A plea won't be necessary," David whispered. He cleared his throat, repeated it. "Soon, you'll get the word that my father is dead. Killed in a prison fight."

Jake walked closer so he could see David's face. "How do you know that?"

David released a long, weary breath. "Because I'm the one who arranged for him to die."

Chapter Nineteen

Jake paced. He wasn't good at waiting, and he pretty much sucked at it when it came to waiting on news about his daughter. Now, he could add Maggie to that list. Sunny was in one room with a team of specialists who were doing the transplant at the Amarillo hospital. Maggie was in another room being treated for the injuries she got from Wade.

This sure as heck wasn't the way to spend Christmas morning.

"Wade," Jake spit out. It was a good thing the weasel was in jail or Jake might be inclined to beat him senseless. The fool had nearly gotten Maggie killed.

"How much longer?" Chet snarled. He was sitting in one of the chairs in the waiting room, but he looked just as impatient as Jake.

Even Nell's nerves were showing. She was next to Chet, a paperback in her hand, but her eyes were fixed on the corridor where they'd last seen both Sunny's and Maggie's doctors.

Royce was the only one not in wait mode. He was on his cell getting updates on the nightmare that Tanner had created when he'd arranged the ambush at the Mustang Ridge hospital. Royce had already relayed that the explosive device was off David and that Billy had him locked up, pending arrival of the Texas Rangers. Jake had gladly handed over jurisdiction to them since he was way too personally involved in the case.

Sheriff Shawn Marcus was okay, too. He'd sustained a gunshot wound to the shoulder and would spend a few days in the hospital, but he was expected to make a full recovery.

And the latest update—one of the ranch hands was on the way to the hospital with Sunny's Christmas presents.

"The transplant has to work," Nell said, and it was something they were all thinking.

While Jake was saying his prayers for Sunny, he was adding some for Maggie, too. She hadn't appeared to be hurt badly, but she'd been in the examining room a long time now.

Royce ended his latest call, and they all looked at him, waiting.

"It's true," Royce said. "Tanner's dead."

None of them reacted. At first. Then, Nell let out a breath of relief. Chet bobbed his head in approval. Jake felt the relief, as well. Tanner had been responsible for so many horrible things, and he hadn't deserved to live.

"David will be charged with murder for hire for his father's death," Royce added. He sank down in the chair next to Nell. "But he's confessed and said he won't fight any of the charges. He'll accept whatever sentence the D.A. offers him."

Good. That would mean no trial, and maybe Jake, his family and Maggie could wash their hands of the Tanners.

"David told Billy that Tanner lured Maggie and you to the prison so he could set up the attack on the road," Royce explained.

Not a surprise, but Jake wanted to kick himself for falling for it. He'd been so desperate to keep Sunny and Maggie safe that he'd made too many mistakes. And Tanner had nearly succeeded in finishing Maggie off.

The sound of the footsteps in the corridor brought all of them to their feet. Not one of the doctors but a nurse. She had something in her hand, but Jake focused on her expression. She wasn't exactly smiling.

Oh, God.

Sunny and Maggie had to be all right.

"Your daughter's fine," the nurse said before she even made it to them. According to her name tag, she was Mary Dickson. "The doctors are very optimistic this will work."

The relief that Jake had felt over Tanner's death was a drop in the bucket compared to what he felt now. He didn't whoop for joy, but he would later. Once his legs weren't so rubbery. He didn't want to disgrace himself by falling flat on his face.

"When can we see her?" Nell asked.

"Soon," Mary assured them with a smile. "The doctor's finishing up now."

More good news, but Jake shook his head. "What about Maggie?"

The nurse's smile vanished, and she handed Jake the folded piece of paper she had in her hand.

Jake's heart went to his knees. "What the hell happened? Is Maggie okay?" And he would have torn past the nurse if she hadn't caught him.

"Ms. Gallagher said the note would explain everything."

Jake looked down at the paper. A note? Maggie had left him a note? "Where is she?" Jake demanded.

Mary shook her head. "She didn't say, but I think if you read the note, you'll know."

He flipped the paper open so quickly that he was surprised it didn't rip in half. Jake hadn't intended to read it aloud, but the words just popped out of his mouth.

Jake, the doctor just told me that Sunny is going to be okay. Thank you for allowing me to help her, and thank you for giving me this time with Sunny and you. If you need more marrow harvested, just contact Marshal Walker. I won't be going back to WITSEC, but he'll know how to reach me. If I stay in Mustang Ridge, it'll only cause problems for you and your family, so I'm saying goodbye. Love, Maggie.

Hell. She was leaving. She wasn't even giving him a chance to tell her how he felt about her.

Except Jake didn't know how he felt.

He cursed, rethought that. Yeah, he did. He knew exactly how he felt, and he wasn't just going to stand there and let Maggie leave.

The nurse cleared her throat. "Maggie said to give you the note in half an hour so she'd have time to get out of the hospital. But I didn't think the part about waiting was a good idea. Hope I'm right about that."

"She's still here?" And Jake couldn't ask that fast enough.

"Maybe." She fluttered her hand toward the back parking lot. "One of the medics is giving her a ride to the police station. They'll be in a white four-door Ford."

Jake turned to run toward the parking lot, but he paused to look at his father. "I want Maggie," he managed to say.

His father's mouth tightened. Then, relaxed a little. "Hell, I could have told you that. Go ahead. Go after her. I won't stand in your way."

Royce and Nell added their nods of approval, and Jake took off. But the truth was, he would have run after Maggie even without his family's approval. Sunny had already given her endorsement by asking Maggie to move to the ranch and be her mommy. That and his feelings for Maggie were all that he needed.

He ran down the corridor toward the parking lot, and he threw open the door. Because the snow was coming down hard now and everything was white, it took him a moment to pick through the lot and the sea of cars to find the Ford. Finally, he spotted her about to get into the passenger's seat. The other woman, the medic no doubt, was already behind the wheel.

"Maggie?" he called out.

She turned, met his gaze, which was possibly a glare. He was mad enough for one. But his glare and anger softened a lot when he saw the bruises on her face, and her moving as if she was still in pain.

"Where do you think you're going?" Jake barreled off the steps and hurried through the snow toward her.

"Amarillo P.D. A marshal is on the way to pick me up."

"And take you where?" he snapped.

She lifted her shoulder, shook her head. And reached for the door handle.

"Not back to the Tip Top Diner," he snarled. Jake made it to her and latched on to her wrist to stop her from opening the door.

"No," she verified. "I'm not sure where I'm going, but I just know I need to get there."

He didn't like the sound of that, and she wasn't exactly rushing into his arms. "Tanner's dead," he told her. "Another prisoner killed him."

She blew out a short breath that mixed with the cold air. "I thought maybe David was telling the truth."

Since she kept dodging his gaze, Jake turned her toward him. "The danger's over, Maggie. You don't have to leave."

"But I do," she argued. "I have to find a life, Jake. I want to be a cop again. I need something, well, normal."

Normal? Well, hell, he wasn't sure he could give her that, but he could do something about the other part. "I've had an opening for another deputy for months now. You're hired if you want it."

She looked at him as if he'd just sprouted a third eye.

"Maggie?" the medic said, lowering the window on the passenger's side. "Are you leaving, or what?"

"Or what," Jake answered for her. "Come back inside and let's talk," he whispered to Maggie.

She glanced around as if trying to decide what to do, but Jake didn't want to see indecision in her eyes. So, he kissed her. He kept it gentle because of those bruises, but he slid his arm around her, pulled her to him and he really kissed her.

He felt her hesitation. And then he didn't. Maggie gripped his arms and returned the kiss. Man, did she. When she finally pulled back, both of them were fighting for air.

"Sheez." She scrubbed her hands down his arms. "You're freezing. Where's your coat?"

"In the waiting room. When I read your note, I ran out without it. That was a stupid note, by the way. And you're stupid to have written it."

Her left eyebrow came up. "Gee, that's just what a girl wants to hear."

Hell. He was messing this up. "You're stronger than that. And what do you care how my family feels about you?"

"I care because you care. You love them."

"Yeah. But this is my life, not theirs." He ducked down, looked at the medic. "If Maggie needs a ride to the police station, I'll take her."

The woman waited for Maggie to give a verifying nod, and she killed the engine and locked up before heading back inside. Jake got Maggie moving in that direction, too. Even though she had on a coat, a huge one that she'd obviously borrowed from someone, it was too cold to be standing in a parking lot. Hard to win an argument with his teeth chattering.

And this was one argument he'd win.

He kept his steps short and slow. "Are you in pain?"

"My hip's a little sore, but I'm okay."

He still didn't speed up. "I'm taking back my *don't*."

She stopped, stared at him. "What?"

"My *don't*." He got them moving again. "When you told me you were falling for me, and I said 'don't.' Well, I'm taking it back."

"Are you saying you want me to fall for you?" she asked.

"Oh, yeah." And he didn't hesitate.

Maggie, however, swallowed hard, and he didn't care for the doubts in her eyes. "My family won't stand in the way," he promised her. "So, if you're looking for an out so you can leave, don't use them."

Her gaze snapped to his. "I don't want an out. I want you. I've loved you since I was fifteen."

Those words alone nearly brought him to his knees. The kiss that followed probably would have, too, if he hadn't heard someone call out his name. It was Nell, and she was standing in the hospital doorway motioning for them.

"Sunny's asking for you," she said. "Both of you."

That got Maggie and him moving even faster.

"She's fine," Nell added. "Better than fine. She already looks like she's getting better. She just wants to see you."

"After we see Sunny," he whispered to Maggie, "I want you to repeat that part about loving me."

And he'd say some things to her that he needed to say.

Maggie and he made their way back into the building and down the corridor to Sunny's room. One look at his baby girl, and he knew Nell had been right. Sunny looked more alert than he'd seen her in weeks, and she gave him a thousand-watt smile when she saw them.

"Daddy and Aunt Maggie." She reached for them, and the nurse quickly handed them some antiseptic wipes for them to use.

Maybe they wouldn't need to take such measures too much longer. He went to Sunny and kissed her on the forehead.

"Santa left your presents at the ranch, but someone's bringing them out. You up to opening them?" Jake asked.

She eagerly bobbed her head and extended her arms to Maggie so it became a group hug. But Sunny's smile faded when she saw the bruises on Maggie's face.

"You got hurt." Sunny sounded very concerned.

"Just a little. And you know how I helped you get better?" Maggie asked. "Well, you're helping me get better."

"How?" Sunny asked.

"By smiling." Maggie gave Sunny's ear a playful tug. "The doctor said that's what will cure my boo-boos. I just need some Sunny smiles."

She giggled, smiled, and Jake figured that sound was the cure for a lot of things. He could almost feel the dark cloud lifting.

Sunny looked up at Maggie. "Are you one of my presents?"

Maggie froze, a surprised sound rattling in her throat. Jake knew what Sunny was asking, and even though he'd wanted to have a talk with Maggie first, he really wanted Sunny to get that present.

"I'm working on that," he assured Sunny. And he turned to Maggie, kissed her. Maybe the kiss would make her a little mindless, as it was doing to him. "I asked Aunt Maggie to stay."

"And what did she say?" Sunny asked.

Both Jake and Sunny stared at Maggie. He hated to put her on the spot like this, but he'd hate even more if she walked out.

Maggie drew in a deep breath and another one when she turned and saw Nell, Royce and Chet in the doorway. "I've loved your daddy for a long time," she said to Sunny. "So, I really want to stay if that's all right with you?"

"And be my mommy?" Sunny pressed.

Jake held his breath. Turned to Maggie. "Will you marry me?" He wondered how many other men had proposed in front of a three-year-old and his entire family.

Maggie blinked. Behind them, he heard his family mumbling. At least there wasn't any profanity, and Royce even said, "All right."

"You want to marry me for Sunny?" Maggie clarified.

"No." Jake put his arm around her, eased her to him. Kissed her. "I want to marry you because I'm in love with you."

The air seemed to swoosh out of her, and Maggie practically collapsed against him. It took Jake a moment, one terrifying moment, to realize she was smiling and relieved.

"Yes, yes, yes," Maggie said. She kissed him back and kept kissing him until Nell cleared her throat.

"Might want to save that for later," Nell suggested.

That was a great idea. Jake wanted lots of *later* with Maggie.

He looked down at Sunny, who was smiling from ear to ear. "I got my Christmas present." Her voice was little, but it showed every bit of her happiness.

"And I got mine," Jake whispered back to her. He brushed another kiss on her forehead.

A nurse made her way through Royce and the others, and she snagged Jake's gaze. "Sunny should probably take a nap before her other presents get here. We don't want her to get too tired."

"Aw, I gotta take a nap?" Sunny complained.

That complaint was music to his ears. It was probably too early for the marrow to be working, but it was a good start to having Sunny nap whether she wanted to or not.

Maggie kissed the top of Sunny's head. "Maybe just a short nap," she bargained. "Close your eyes, and when you wake up, there'll be more presents. Lots and lots of them."

Sunny closed her eyes but then peeked out. "Next Christmas I want a baby sister."

Jake didn't know who was more shocked by that—Maggie, him or Chet.

"I'll see what I can do about that," Jake told his daughter.

"A baby sister?" Royce teased as they filed back into the hall and the nurse closed the door. He looked at Maggie. "You think Jake's up for that?"

"He is," Jake answered for her. "But I figure I need to get a ring on her finger first."

"I can help with that." Nell took the diamond ring from her hand and tried to hand it to Maggie. "It was Mom's engagement ring."

Maggie pushed Nell's hand away. "I couldn't take your mother's ring."

"Sure you can," Nell said at the same moment that Royce said, "Why not?"

"Since Jake's the oldest, Mother would have wanted his wife to have it," Nell insisted. She leaned in, kissed Maggie's cheek. "Welcome to the family."

"Yeah, welcome," Royce added, and he kissed her, too.

"Here," Nell said, handing the ring to Jake. "Get it on her fast before she changes her mind." Nell winked at him and Maggie.

Even though he didn't think there'd be any mind-changing today, Jake did take Maggie's hand, and he slipped the ring onto her finger. Perfect fit.

Tears sprang to her eyes, and she practically melted into him. Jake was ready to give her another of those celebration kisses, but he realized one person hadn't given them well-wishes, and that one person—his father—was staring at them.

"Don't you dare object," Royce ordered Chet.

That caused Chet to bristle. "Wasn't going to object. I was just gonna say I'd rather have a grandson next time around. Especially since it appears neither Nell nor you is interested in getting me another generation to help run the ranch."

And with that, Chet turned and headed toward the waiting room.

"Coming from him, that's practically a whoop for joy," Jake assured Maggie.

She laughed and then gave him a look that let him know she, too, would like one of those celebratory kisses. Nell and Royce picked up on that, and they mumbled something about checking on the Christmas presents.

Maggie watched as Chet disappeared around the corner. "I want to marry you. More than my next breath, I want that, but I don't think living under the same roof with Chet would be a good idea."

Jake had a simple solution for that. "Then, we won't. I own all that land by the creek, and we can break ground there for a new house."

"You'd build me a house?" she asked, surprised.

"I'd build *us* a house. You, me and Sunny."

She smiled, inched him closer to her. "And you'd offer me a job?"

"That, too. But you'd have to sleep with the boss." And since Jake was the boss, he hoped she wouldn't object.

Her smile widened, and she inched even closer. "Before or after I take the job?"

"Both."

"I like the sound of that. In fact, I like the sound of all of it—you, the house, the job, a new life with Sunny and you."

"So do I."

And Jake meant it with all his heart.

He pulled her to him and gave her the kiss that they'd both been wanting. Not just to celebrate but to seal the deal of their becoming a family.

"Merry Christmas, Maggie."

Next month, don't miss USA TODAY *bestselling author*
Delores Fossen's
STANDOFF AT MUSTANG RIDGE.
Look for it wherever
Harlequin Intrigue books are sold!

COMING NEXT MONTH from Harlequin® Intrigue®
AVAILABLE JANUARY 2, 2013

#1395 STANDOFF AT MUSTANG RIDGE
Delores Fossen

After a one-night stand with bad boy Deputy Royce McCall, Texas heiress Sophie Conway might be pregnant with Royce's baby. And the possible pregnancy has unleashed a killer.

#1396 NATIVE COWBOY
Bucking Bronc Lodge
Rita Herron

When a selfless pregnant doctor becomes the target of a ruthless serial killer, she has no choice but to turn to the man who walked away from her months ago...the father of her child.

#1397 SOLDIER'S REDEMPTION
The Legacy
Alice Sharpe

Cole Bennett is at an impossible impasse: seek the truth of his past, though it threatens to destroy any chance of a future with the woman he loves, or turn away....

#1398 ALPHA ONE
Shadow Agents
Cynthia Eden

If Juliana James wants to stay alive, then she must trust navy SEAL Logan Quinn. But trusting Logan isn't easy...he's the man who broke her heart ten years before.

#1399 INTERNAL AFFAIRS
Alana Matthews

When Sheriff's Deputy Rafe Franco answers a callout on a domestic dispute, he has no idea that he's about to step into his past...and into the arms of the woman he had once loved.

#1400 BRIDAL FALLS RANCH RANSOM
Jan Hambright

Eve Brooks's beautiful face was erased by an explosion alongside a dark highway. But with former FBI agent J. P. Ryker's help, can she discover her inner beauty and strength before her tormenter strikes again?

If thrilling romances and heart-racing action is what you're after, then check out Harlequin Romantic Suspense!

NEW LOOK COMING DEC 18!

Featuring bold women, unforgettable men and the life-and-death situations that bring them together, these stories deliver!

SNEAK
PEEK

COWBOY WITH A CAUSE
by Carla Cassidy

Turn the page for a sneak peek at the latest book
in the Cowboy Café miniseries

COMING JANUARY 2013!

Look for the latest title from best-loved veteran
series author Carla Cassidy

When rancher Adam Benson rents a room from the
wheechair-bound Melanie Brooks, he finds himself not only
a part of her healing process, but discovers he's the only man
who stands between her and a deranged killer....

Read on for an excerpt from

COWBOY WITH A CAUSE

Available January 2013 from Harlequin
Romantic Suspense

There was no way in hell he wanted the sheriff or any of the
deputies seeing Melanie in her sexy blue nightgown. He found
the white terry cloth robe just where she'd told him it would
be and carried it back into her bedroom with him. He helped
her into it and then wrapped his arms around her.

The idea that anyone would try to put their hands on her in
an effort to harm her shot rage through him.

"I didn't do this to myself," she whispered.

He leaned back and looked at her in surprise. "It never
crossed my mind that you did."

"Maybe somebody will think I'm just some poor crippled
woman looking for attention, that I tore the screen off the
window, left my wheelchair in the corner and then crawled
into the closet and waited for you to come home." A new sob
welled up and spilled from her lips.

"Melanie…stop," he protested.

She looked up at him with eyes that simmered with emotion. "Isn't that what you think? That I'm just a poor little cripple?"

"Never," he replied truthfully. "And you need to get that thought out of your head. We need to get you into the living room. The sheriff should be here anytime."

She swiped at the tears that had begun to fill her eyes once again. "Can you bring me my chair?"

He started for it and then halted in his tracks. "We need to leave it where it is. Maybe there are fingerprints on it that will let us know who was in here."

He walked back to where she sat on the bed and scooped her up in his arms. Once again, she wrapped her arms around his neck and leaned into him. For a moment he imagined that he could feel her heartbeat matching the rhythm of his own.

"It's going to be all right, Melanie," he promised. "I'm here and I'm going to make sure everything is all right." He just hoped it was a promise he could keep.

**Will Melanie ride off into the sunset with her sexy
new live-in cowboy? Or will a murderous lunatic,
lurking just a breath away, add another victim
to his tally? Find out what happens next in**

COWBOY WITH A CAUSE

**Available January 2013 only from Harlequin
Romantic Suspense wherever books are sold.**